Summer Vacation

MURDER

BONZAI
MOON

BonzaiMoon Books LLC
Houston, Texas
www.bonzaimoonbooks.com

1

An icy jolt passed through Roland "Beanie" Bean, chilling him even though the humid air was north of ninety degrees and the winds gusting from the ocean were as hot as the mid-afternoon sun.

A few seconds earlier, as his young son Ethan sprinted toward the Olympic-sized swimming pool, Beanie suspected what the sneaky little rascal was planning. Sure enough, when Ethan vaulted in the air, arms hugged around his knees, which were pressed against his chest, Beanie thought, *cannonball*.

Beanie held his breath as Ethan crashed into the pool, sending a tidal wave of water into the air, drenching the other kiddos who giggled and squealed in delight. The pool attendants assigned with the task of entertaining a gaggle of hyperactive kids jumped away from the spray but remained diligent in their assignment, making sure the kids were okay. Beanie was relieved that Ethan's stunt hadn't resulted in tears, tantrums, or any other trauma. On the contrary, the other children surrounded Ethan as he dog paddled, demanding that he do another cannonball. Thankfully, the pool attendants were quick to squash that idea, suggesting instead a game of Marco Polo.

Sighing in relief, Beanie eased back into the chaise where he lounged, ten feet from the edge of the pool where four-year-old Ethan and two-year-old Evan were having the time of their lives in the freshwater. Pool time was one of the many supervised activities designed to engage children so their parents didn't have to entertain them, according to the Children's Coordinator, a spunky, fresh-faced young woman who'd met with them hours after their arrival at Aerie Islands Spa Club.

Glancing around, Beanie couldn't help being impressed, and somewhat intimidated, by the luxurious, posh surroundings. Aerie Islands Spa Club was a far cry from the community clubhouse and pool in the modest, working-class neighborhood of Oyster Farms, where he, his wife, and their boys lived on the island of St. Killian. Located in the Aerie Islands, an archipelago roughly thirty miles west of the Palmchat Islands, where Beanie and his family lived, the Aerie Islands Spa Club was an enclave for the rich and famous.

Being neither rich nor famous, Beanie felt like a fish out of water.

All around him, wealthy and fabulous members of the one percent milled about in sun-drenched luxury, lost in a blissful fog of apathy and laziness, giving their attention to afternoon cocktails and inconsequential conversation.

Beanie took a deep breath and tried not to feel out of place. And yet, he was. The Aerie Islands Spa Club wasn't a place he could afford to take his family. Not even in his wildest dreams could he have ever imagined vacationing in such a glamorous destination. Lucky for him, he didn't have to conjure up any wild dreams. All he'd had to do was accept the generous offer of his boss, Leo Bronson, the owner, and publisher of the *Palmchat Gazette*, where Beanie worked as an investigative reporter.

After casually mentioning his desire to take his wife and kids to a nice resort for a two-week summer vacation, Beanie's immediate supervisor, Leo's wife, Vivian Thomas-Bronson, the newspaper's Managing Editor, casually mentioned that Leo's father, the publishing magnate Burt Bronson, was part owner of Aerie Islands Spa Club.

"Leo's dad has a villa. It's beyond fabulous," Vivian had told him. "You should take Noelle and the boys there."

Initially, Beanie balked at the idea.

He'd heard of Aerie Islands Spa Club. A private resort community of palatial villas, it was built along the uneven slope of a lush, verdant mountain overlooking the coastal town of Amargo, the island capital. The resort boasted an elite, exclusive membership that included European royalty, foreign dignitaries and diplomats, former presidents, Russian oligarchs, A-list celebrities, and an assortment of various and sundry billionaires.

Beanie knew he couldn't afford to take his family there.

Vivian made it clear that the trip would be a gift, but Beanie still wasn't sure. He didn't want to feel like a charity case. Vivian must have sensed his reluctance because she encouraged him to think of the offer as a bonus. Or an employee benefit. A reward for a job well done, considering the number of stories he'd written that had trended.

And yet, Beanie remained on the fence.

His wife Noelle, had not.

"Roland, do not even think of turning down Vivian's offer," warned Noelle.

And so, here his family of four was, enjoying the lush life. Two days into their two-week sojourn, the boys were having the time of their lives. Noelle was loving being pampered, partaking in a myriad of spa treatments and wellness activities. And Beanie was—

"… relaxing?"

Jarred from his reverie, Beanie glanced up.

Smiling, looking pretty, and smelling like jasmine, sage, and lemon, Noelle sat on the chaise next to Beanie's and stretched out on the plush cushions.

"What?" asked Beanie.

"I said, I thought you were supposed to be relaxing," said Noelle.

"I am relaxing," said Beanie.

Noelle gave him a dubious side-eye. "Then why do you look so tense?"

"Well, I was about to relax, but …"

"But?"

Glancing toward the pool, Beanie said, "But Ethan did a cannonball into the pool."

Laughing, Noelle said, "Why am I not surprised?"

"I'm not sure, but I'm surprised," said Beanie, looking at his wife, wondering what kind of treatment had suppressed her helicopter parenting tendencies.

"Surprised about what?" asked Noelle, accepting a mimosa from one of the many attendants traversing the pool area carrying pastel-colored cocktails on silver trays.

Passing on a libation, Beanie said, "I would have thought you'd be upset about Ethan's antics. Cannonballing is against the rules. And dangerous."

Noelle took a sip of her drink. "True, but I'm on vacation. I refuse to smother."

Beanie was glad to hear that. Normally, Noelle was over-protective to the point of being a bit overbearing. She fretted and worried about the boys and didn't apologize for hovering. It was odd to think of her being so laissez-faire toward her kids.

The weird thing was that Beanie felt forgotten and neglected when he saw his boys excited and delighted by the pool coordinators, two sun-kissed and athletic young women leading the children in the Marco Polo game. He was a hands-on father, accustomed to horseplaying and roughhousing with his kids at the beach. The other parents were the type to leave the actual parenting of children to nannies, au pairs, caretakers, governesses, and other members of their vast armies of staff. Beanie wanted to be in the pool, laughing and playing with his boys, not lazing around, thankful he didn't have to deal with them.

"Look at you looking fabulous!"

Glancing toward the festive, musical voice, Beanie gave a wave to the woman walking toward their semi-private cabana. Carmen Taylor, the head wellness coordinator, had a bright smile, caramel complexion, and a short haircut that always reminded Beanie of the Disney character Tinkerbell. Dressed in a coral-colored shirtdress, the official uniform of the resort's administrative staff, Carmen was trim, petite, and had the pleasant attitude of someone whose job was to defer to entitled guests and de-escalate situations before things got out of control.

Carmen and Noelle, who'd gone to secondary school together before Noelle left the Palmchat Islands to attend high school in America, had been delighted to reconnect and, thus far, had spent a fair amount of time catching up when Carmen took breaks from her busy schedule.

Laughing, Noelle said, "Thanks to your recommendation."

"I told you the volcanic ash, sea kelp, and sand body polish treatment would have your skin glowing," said Carmen, taking a seat at the small bistro table positioned between the chaises. "Not that your skin needed any help to glow. It was already beautiful."

Beanie agreed. His wife was a bona fide stunner. Noelle didn't need spa treatments to look good. Still, Beanie believed the pampering had relaxed her. As a busy mom of two with a stressful job as a pharmacist, Noelle deserved some self-care and "me" time.

"You guys should do the couples' aromatherapy, mud bath, and hot stone massage," said Carmen.

"Roland, that sounds wonderful," said Noelle, rising to a sitting position. "Don't you think?"

"I probably could use a massage," admitted Beanie.

"You do look a bit tense," commented Carmen.

"That's because of our four-year-old, Ethan," said Noelle. "He broke some of the pool rules."

Waving a dismissive hand, Carmen said, her voice lowered, "Don't worry about that. All these rich kids who come here break the rules and get away with it. All day. Every day. Having money means you don't have to listen to instructions or suffer consequences of your bad behavior."

"Well, Ethan is not a rich kid," pointed out Beanie as he glanced toward the pool. On one end, little Evan, wearing floaties on his chubby arms, sat with a few other toddlers in the kiddie pool, all of them laughing and clapping along with the assistant who led them in some sort of water game. On the opposite end, Ethan had taken over the Marco Polo challenge, which didn't seem to bother the two female pool workers. As the four-to-six-year-olds played, they engaged in what appeared to be a rather intense conversation with lots of head shaking and frowns.

Near the center of the pool was the tall lifeguard's chair, manned by a strapping, muscular young guy who seemed to be paying more attention than the two additional lifeguards hanging out a few feet away. Like the young female pool attendants, the lifeguards were talking and joking around, occasionally shoving each other, and sometimes checking their phones.

"And Ethan can be a handful sometimes," added Noelle, finishing her mimosa.

"Sometimes?" Beanie chuckled under his breath. "Try all of the time."

"Honey, enjoy them at that age for as long as you can," advised Carmen. "Before you know it, they'll be teenagers, and then it's all downhill from there."

"Is it?" asked Beanie.

"Why do you say that?" asked Noelle, her voice laced with curiosity and concern.

Carmen sighed. "I say that because of my son, Marcus … that's him over there at the lifeguard booth."

Beanie glanced over. Of the two lifeguards horsing around, he figured Marcus was the young man who shared Carmen's complexion and her wide smile.

"I got him this job to keep him out of trouble," said Carmen. "Doesn't seem to have worked."

"What do you mean?" asked Beanie, focusing on Carmen.

"I swear that boy has gone from the frying pan into the fire," said Carmen. "Once again, he's falling in with the wrong crowd."

"Which is?" asked Beanie.

"The pool crew," said Carmen, tension tightening her facial features. "The lifeguards, Pablo—he's the one on duty now—and the other one, Seth."

Beanie glanced toward Marcus again. Seth had to be the sunburned blonde Marcus was clowning around with when he should have been working. Pablo, the muscular guy in the lifeguard chair, was of mixed heritage. Possibly West Indian, Portuguese, and European, but with Latin features and an olive complexion.

"Plus, those two girls with Ethan's group," said Carmen, inclining her head in the direction of the young women, who were paying slightly more attention to the kids now. "One of whom is very loose—if you know what I mean."

Beanie did, but it didn't particularly bother him. As a teenager, he'd known a few "loose" girls himself, much to his mother's chagrin. When he looked at Noelle, Beanie was surprised to find her expression sanguine. Maybe she was still under the spell of volcanic ash and sea kelp. He thought Noelle might be horrified, imagining Ethan and Evan as randy teen boys chasing flirty girls.

"The pool crew, that's what they call themselves," said Carmen, "is nothing but trouble. I've heard all sorts of things from other staff, and some of the guests."

Noelle asked, "Like what?"

"Relations in the empty guest villas," said Carmen, lips pursed. "Late night parties, drinking, drugs. Worst of all is the allegations of stealing. Some of the guests have reported expensive valuables missing, mainly jewels, clothes."

"And Marcus is involved in all the … trouble?" asked Beanie.

"He swears to me he's not," said Carmen. "But I found a joint in the trash can in his bathroom. He claimed it didn't belong to him. Said Pablo or Seth must have tossed it in the trash. I told him, in no uncertain terms, that I did not want him having anything to do with anyone doing drugs. And yet, there he is, hanging around Seth and Pablo."

"Well, he works with them," started Beanie, but he trailed off when Carmen gave him a sharp look.

Stung by the woman's nonverbal rebuke, Beanie cleared his throat.

Noelle said, "Considering the trouble I caused my mom when I was sixteen, I can't throw stones. And my boys are four and two, so I can't give any advice, but—"

"Oh, no, honey, I just needed to rant," said Carmen, standing. "And I shouldn't be complaining when you two should be relaxing."

"We don't mind listening," said Noelle. "We're here whenever you need to talk."

Nodding, Carmen said, "Anyway, I'll book that couples massage and email you the details."

Moments after Carmen walked away, Beanie looked at his wife. "You really amaze me."

Noelle laughed. "What? Why?"

"Well, Carmen was going on and on about her son getting into trouble with fast girls and drugs and stealing," said Beanie. "You didn't seem worried that we might have problems like that with Ethan and Evan."

"Ha!" said Noelle as she settled back on the lounge chair. "Talk to me in ten years. I'll be a pearl-clutching, hand-wringing, basket case by then, trust me."

"Aw, you won't be that bad," said Beanie, though he suspected his wife would be much worse, and prayed the ten years would not speed by.

"I'm just hoping that neither Ethan nor Evan will follow in my footsteps," said Noelle, closing her eyes.

"Follow in your footsteps?"

"The apple doesn't fall far from the tree," said Noelle.

"Elle, what are you talking about?" asked Beanie, but he had a feeling she meant those wayward teen years she'd alluded to during their conversation with Carmen. His wife's past—which he hadn't been aware of and had discovered accidentally—had been marked by danger and violence. Noelle had moved beyond that tumultuous time in her life, and was now a wonderful wife and mother, and had a successful career. But there were moments when Beanie suspected his wife was still haunted and ashamed of her background. Noelle believed her bad decisions had somehow been genetic, considering that her father was Josue Chartres—a fearsome former assassin for the PC-5, a notorious Caribbean cartel.

Recently, Noelle's father, serving a life sentence without the possibility of parole at Tiverton, a maximum-security island prison, had expressed interest in a relationship with his grandsons. Noelle was staunchly opposed to any form of communication or connection between the boys and Josue. His wife probably feared the kids might be negatively influenced to take up a life of crime, but Beanie didn't think—

" … not even paying attention," growled a thick baritone with a hint of a slur. "One of those kids is going to drown …"

"No one is going to drown," was the clipped reply from an irritated female voice. "Why would you say something so awful?"

Frowning at the voices, Beanie tried to discern where they were coming from. Out of nowhere, they floated from his left. When he turned his head, a row of large hibiscus bushes, used to provide privacy between the cabanas, prevented him from seeing the people speaking.

"It's not awful, it's the truth," said the man. "They hire these punk kids and pay them more money than they deserve to fool around and not do their jobs!"

"No one is fooling around and not doing their jobs," disputed the woman.

Squinting, Beanie could just make out shapes between the dense leaves and vibrant, fuchsia petals.

"Well, of course, you're going to defend the lifeguard …"

"Excuse me?"

"Don't pretend …"

"What are you talking about?"

Beanie wondered, as well, what the man, obviously drunk, was talking about. And yet, he scolded himself for wondering. He was on vacation. Not on assignment. He shouldn't be eavesdropping. Then again, he wasn't listening on purpose. The couple was talking and he could hear what they were saying. But he shouldn't have been paying attention. Like his wife, he needed to relax.

"I've seen you flirting with him …"

"Flirting with who?" demanded the woman. "What are you talking about?"

"That lifeguard," slurred the man. "I saw you smiling and batting your eyelashes at him."

"Batting my eyelashes?" The woman scoffed. "You really shouldn't drink before five."

"You really shouldn't flirt with the help," said the man. "Especially a young guy who's half your age."

"I was being friendly," snapped the woman. "You should try it sometimes!"

"Roland ..."

Jumping slightly, Beanie glanced toward Noelle, giving him a curious look.

"What's going on?" whispered his wife. "Who is that talking?"

His voice lowered, Beanie said, "No idea. Man and woman in the cabana next to ours. Having some kind of argument."

Noelle frowned. "Argument?"

"About the lifeguard."

"Marcus?" asked Noelle.

"I don't know," admitted Beanie. "Maybe—"

"Hey! You! Yeah ... you!" shouted the man from the adjacent cabana. "I'm gonna report you!"

"Oh my God, will you please sit down!" The woman said, her voice laced with annoyance and mortification. "You are embarrassing yourself!"

Seconds later, the man stomped toward the edge of the pool, allowing Beanie a view of the person whose voice he'd overheard. Dressed in wrinkled swim shorts, he was short and barrel-chested. Most likely middle-aged, he had thinning hair, saggy jowls, and leathery, sun-mottled skin. Apropos of nothing, Beanie had the urge to recommend the volcanic ash and sea kelp treatment. As he'd suspected, the man was inebriated, as evidenced by his stumbling gait.

"Does your boss know you aren't doing your job?" asked the man from the cabana, pointing an accusing finger toward the lifeguard chair. Beanie noticed there had been a shift change. Seth, the blonde, was now sitting in the lifeguard seat while Marcus and Pablo were hanging out, standing near the pool's edge.

"What is happening?" asked Noelle.

Beanie shook his head. He wasn't sure, but at once, there was tension in the air, like a negative charge. Polarized and silenced, the other guests became attuned to the unfolding drama, abandoning their laughter, conversations, and libations. Even the kids had stopped giggling. The waitstaff was frozen.

"I saw you up in that chair! You weren't paying attention!" The man from the cabana stomped around the edge of the pool, heading in the direction of Marcus and Pablo, who both seemed confused. "Somebody could have drowned and you wouldn't have even known it!"

"Fred, please, stop!" cried a woman who ran out of the cabana where the drunk man had been. Following him, she called out for him to cease his rude, rowdy behavior, but the drunk man—Fred—ignored her. Continuing his tirade against the lifeguard, Pablo, the drunk brute lumbered around the pool, slipping and stumbling.

The other guests watched and whispered among themselves but made no effort to stop Fred from confronting Pablo.

"They should have fired you a long time ago!" thundered Fred, wobbling closer to Pablo. "They never should have hired you! Don't deserve this job!"

In response, Pablo folded his arms across his muscled chest and smirked at Fred.

"I'm gonna talk to your boss!" threatened Fred, stabbing a finger up toward Pablo, who was a foot taller than him. "Tell him he's paying you for nothing!"

"Fred, will you stop it!" seethed the woman—his wife, Beanie assumed—who grabbed his arm and tried to pull him away.

Yanking away from his wife, Fred threw an uncoordinated punch at Pablo, who didn't need to duck as the fist came nowhere near him. Jabbing the air, Fred lost his balance, stumbled, and whirled himself from the edge of the pool into the water.

A chorus of gasps and giggles broke out as Fred broke the surface, spitting water and sputtering curses. Seconds later, three beefy men in linen suits and sunglasses with walkie-talkies and earpieces appeared out of nowhere to lift Fred from the water. Despite his yelling and cursing, the men had no problem escorting him away from the pool area. Fred's wife followed, quickly covering her pale face with large sunglasses as she slinked away, head lowered, her voluminous silk cover-up billowing behind her.

"Wow …" deadpanned Noelle.

"Exactly," agreed Beanie.

"I think I need another mimosa," announced his wife.

Beanie said, "I think I need something stronger …"

2

According to the brochure, the Aerie Islands Spa Club was more of a small village than a resort.

At least, that was what the founders and developers had desired. It was less of a five-star property and more akin to a posh, exclusive gated community. Among the large villas, most of which were hidden behind towering palms and clusters of flowering privacy bushes and hedges, were a plethora of amenities, including a golf course, tennis and equestrian centers, and various restaurants, bars, and cafes.

At a few minutes past seven in the morning, Beanie took the opportunity to explore the expansive grounds.

Employing one of the villa's four golf carts, he motored along the wide cobblestone paths that wound in and out and around the lush, verdant grounds. With the early morning sunrays at his back and a fragrance of tropical smells surrounding him, Beanie enjoyed the solitude as he came abreast of various Caribbean Colonial buildings. On his right was the gift shop, clothing store, florist, post office, and Children's Center. On his left, there was a health clinic, a business center, and the main administrative offices. Beanie continued as the path meandered through manicured landscaping, brilliant, vibrant hibiscus, and fruit trees interspersed with Oleander bushes, Queen Palms, palmettos, and allspice trees that perfumed the air.

Beyond the vegetation was the large community center, a multi-storied building fronted by a green square and surrounded by a perimeter of palm trees. Inside the imposing building was the main reception area, where Beanie and his family had checked in, and other halls and rooms designed for meeting and socializing.

Heading past the center, Beanie took a path that veered left, toward his destination, the grocery store.

An hour earlier, he'd been jostled awake by Noelle, no longer under the sedative effects of her volcanic ash and sea kelp treatment, who barked instructions with the commanding presence of a military strategist.

He needed to rise and shine, immediately, and following a quick shower, his wife wanted him to go to the village grocery store to buy snacks for their day trip excursion to one of the many sandbars surrounding the Aerie Islands, for which the archipelago was famous.

Beanie glanced at his watch, knowing he couldn't waste time.

Noelle had estimated his trip should take no longer than half an hour. A minute more and his wife would morph into scold mode. Several golf carts were parked in front of the pale pink store when Beanie arrived. He secured a spot next to a shady banyan tree, then hopped out of the cart and strode toward the entrance.

Inside the store, he gave perfunctory waves to a few other guests starting the day early, then nodded at the store attendant, a young island guy dressed in coral shorts and a matching coral polo shirt. The bright, airy space, decorated in a customary West Indian style, featured an array of products on mahogany shelves that formed narrow rows. Along the walls of the store were bookshelves and cabinets interspersed between large, wide jalousie windows, opened to allow sea-scented breezes.

Perusing the shelves, Beanie grew worried. Most of the stock was high-end, luxury items. Parmigiano Reggiano, Wagyu beef, Iberico Ham, Caviar, Free-Range Eggs, truffle oil, Black truffles, Oysters, Kobe Beef, Lobster. Noelle wanted picnic food. Things the boys would eat.

Peanut butter and jelly or shredded goat sandwiches. Plantain and sweet potato chips. Cookies. Apples. Oranges. Bananas.

Beanie sighed as he surveyed the fresh fruit arrayed in wicker baskets. White strawberries. Honey-dipped, hand-pollinated apples. Australian mangos. Roman grapes. Not exactly what his boys would like. And, as he discreetly checked the prices, not exactly what he wanted to pay.

His frustration growing, Beanie crossed the store to a table featuring sandwiches. The offerings were no better, and again, outrageously expensive. Fig, blue cheese, & prosciutto croissant. Buttermilk fried goat and bacon cheddar waffle. Brie & pear grilled cheese. Spiced sweet potato with feta.

"Do you need any assistance with anything, sir?"

Beanie glanced at the store attendant. "You have anything ..."

The attendant lowered his voice and, with a knowing look, said, "Less expensive?"

Frowning, Beanie wondered if it was obvious he didn't belong at the Aerie Islands Spa Club. Could the staff tell he wasn't one of the one percent? Did he look like a regular, average island working stiff? Perhaps he lacked the fresh aroma of money?

Well, he wasn't part of the one percent. And he was an average guy who hired out his labor. He certainly didn't smell like money. Nevertheless, he wasn't sure how he felt about being so quickly recognized as middle class. He wasn't ashamed of his status or station in life, but he didn't want anyone assuming he couldn't afford the store's prices. Because he could. However, a bag of groceries would definitely break the budget.

Beanie said, "Actually, I was going to say anything that two active little boys might be willing to eat."

"Kids eat stuff from here," said the attendant, in a tone Beanie couldn't quite identify. It was smug and yet dismissive, and Beanie had the feeling that the guy was passing judgment against him. Again, Beanie discerned the attendant was telling him, in a sly and subtle way, that he didn't belong.

"My boys are finicky eaters," said Beanie, hating that his explanation felt like an excuse. "We're going to one of the sandbars and—"

"All the sandbars have food stalls," said the attendant. "Simple food and cheap prices."

Beanie fought to ignore his annoyance at the attendant's elitism, which was ridiculous. The guy was working in a grocery store, not staying at the village, Still, Beanie figured he'd just thank the guy. But before he could, Beanie was interrupted by another customer.

"Do you have angulas?"

"Angulas?" asked the attendant, turning his back on Beanie to face the patron with the question.

Beanie had no idea what an angula was, but he recognized the voice of the man who'd asked.

"Do you know what an angula is?" inquired a woman whose voice Beanie knew.

"They're glass noodles," said the man.

"No, actually, they're baby eels from Northern Spain," corrected the woman.

The man said, "After hatching in the Gulf Stream, they grow while they travel on a two-year journey to Europe, where they end up on the shores of Spain."

The woman said, "Such a perilous and tumultuous trip! That's why they're considered a delicacy."

Chuckling to himself, Beanie recalled the first time he'd met the couple, Chuck, and Florence Taylor, wealthy ex-pats who lived a glamourous life in a luxurious, upscale neighborhood in St. Killian. The previous April, Noelle's boss had invited their family to a swanky Easter egg hunt and the Taylor's had been guests. After a dead body had been found during the event, Beanie had solicited the Taylor's help in finding out information about a murder suspect, much to their mischievous delight.

As Chuck and Flo commandeered the store attendant, Beanie contemplated sneaking away. He didn't mind socializing with the couple, but Chuck and Flo tended to hijack time, which Beanie didn't have. A quick check of his watch showed that in five minutes, Noelle would expect to see him walking back into the villa, so—

"Oh, Chuck, is that Beanie?"

"I think it is!"

"Oh, I think you're right! Beanie!"

Busted, Beanie took a quick, deep breath, then turned to face the couple, who greeted him with smiles and hugs and good-natured questions about his presence at the Aerie Islands Spa Club. What was he doing there? Did he have a villa on the island? If so, why didn't he tell them?

"We haven't seen you in forever!"

"It's been much too long!"

Beanie didn't know if he agreed with that, but he said, "Yeah, it has been a while."

"How long are you, your wife, and the girls staying?" asked Flo.

"Two weeks," said Beanie, laughing to himself at Flo's mistake. "But, it's my wife and the boys."

"Flo, how could you forget Beanie's three little boys?" asked Chuck.

"Only two boys," said Beanie, quick to correct Chuck, shuddering to himself at the thought of another rambunctious kid. "Just two."

"Right, right …" said Chuck, nodding as he glanced at his wife, who glanced at him.

Beanie caught the skeptical look that passed between the couple. Chuck and Flo were the types to believe they were right even when proven wrong, but Beanie wasn't irritated. Possibly because his attention was momentarily arrested by the man who'd just walked into the store.

A man he recognized.

The drunk guy at the pool who'd confronted Pablo, the young, good-looking lifeguard. After throwing a wild punch that didn't land, he'd belly-flopped into the pool before being hustled out of the area by a trio of brisk, beefy security guards. What was his name? Fred?

"Flo and I are staying for a week, or so," said Chuck.

"Maybe two," said Flo.

Beanie nodded distractedly as, roughly ten feet away, Fred and the store attendant huddled together, their expressions tense as they conversed near the check-out counter.

"And then we might head to our place in Patagonia," said Chuck.

"Or our house in Monaco," said Flo.

"Or maybe the place we bought in Australia last year," said Chuck.

As the Taylors continued the roll call of their various properties across the globe, Beanie kept an eye on Fred and the store attendant. What were they talking about so intensely? How did they know each other? From Fred's diatribe the day before, he didn't seem the type to mingle with "the help," as he'd referred to the staff.

"Anyway, we'll figure out where we want to go," said Flo, waving a hand in the air, her tone just as airy, typical of someone with more money than she could spend in several lifetimes.

"Speaking of where we want to go," said Chuck, smiling, his expression expansive. "Flo and I are heading to breakfast. Why don't you and your family join us?"

"Oh, what a great idea!" exclaimed Flo.

"Actually, Noelle, the boys, and I are heading to one of the sandbars for a day trip," said Beanie, strangely relieved that his family had plans. "Maybe another time? We are here for two weeks."

Chuck and Flo were disappointed, but understanding.

"Let us know," said Flo. "Text us."

"You have our number," said Chuck.

As Beanie nodded, he caught movement in his periphery, and a slight turn of his head gave him a view of Fred and the store attendant heading away from the front counter. Something about their movements seemed furtive, and their mannerisms secretive.

"Well, I guess they don't have angula," lamented Flo.

Glancing around, Chuck said, "Obviously not."

"Unfortunate," said Flo.

Beanie nodded his sympathy as he walked with the couple toward the door. "I know what you mean. This place doesn't have much that my boys would eat, but I'm going to look around a bit more before I give up."

"Good luck!" said Chuck.

"Tell Nicole, Ernie, and Eddie we said 'hi,'" said Florence as the couple exited the store.

Chuckling his frustration at Flo's seeming unwillingness to get his family's names correct, Beanie turned. To his left, several feet away, toward the back of the store, he spotted the attendant leading Fred into a door with *Employees Only* stenciled on the aqua-painted surface. Beanie scratched his chin. What was that about? Glancing about the store, still occupied by several guests, most of whom perused the aisles with unconcerned leisure, Beanie angled toward the Employees Only door, which was opened slightly.

Grabbing a package of high-end vegan granola from a shelf, Beanie stopped near the aqua-painted door and pretended to read the contents of the product as he strained to listen.

" … you know anybody who can help me out?" asked Fred.

The attendant answered, "I might, but …"

"But … ?"

"But, are you sure this is how you want to handle things?"

"That punk needs to learn that he can't disrespect me," said Fred. "He needs to be taught a lesson."

"The guy I know has ties to the PC-5 …"

A chill sliced through Beanie. Any mention of the dreaded island cartel gave him conflicting feelings. On the one hand, he feared and loathed the tropical mob, which had terrorized the Palmchat Islands with their culture of murder and mayhem. But, on the other, his wife had ties to the gang. Ties that couldn't be severed. Beanie also relied on a PC-5 member as a valued and trusted confidential source. His opinion of the cartel had become more nuanced and harder to reconcile.

"Sounds like the right guy for the job," said Fred.

What job, wondered Beanie.

"What exactly do you want him to do?" asked the store attendant. "I'm asking because his fee varies depending on the particular service rendered …"

Particular service rendered? What was going on? What were they talking about—

Three sharp pokes against his left shoulder startled Beanie. Confused, he glanced back.

A small, elderly woman dressed in tennis whites stared up at him. Beneath the sun visor, her bright blue eyes conveyed hints of irritation.

"Yes …" said Beanie, not quite sure what to think. Did he know this woman? She didn't look familiar. Or maybe she thought she knew him? Or maybe—

"I'm looking for the Pear and Camembert mini platter," said the woman, her low gravelly voice—and the nicotine wafting from her breath—exposing her pack a day smoking habit. "I see the Pear and Blue Cheese, but I don't like blue cheese, however—"

"Oh, um …" Fighting annoyance and embarrassment, Beanie said, "I don't work here."

Giving him a skeptical look, the woman said, "You don't?"

"I can help you, ma'am …" said a crisp, efficient voice behind Beanie, which he recognized. It was the attendant. Beanie turned. The attendant scowled at him before his face morphed into pleasant deference as he maneuvered around Beanie and happily assisted the smoking woman.

As the attendant led the elderly woman down the aisle, Beanie ruminated on the conversation he'd overheard. What was the service Fred needed? Why was a guy with ties to the PC-5 the best person for the job? And who was the punk who needed to be taught a lesson?

Beanie wasn't sure, but he had suspicions …

3

"Are we there, yet, Daddy?" demanded Ethan, for the fifth, or maybe sixth, or maybe fifteenth time.

"No, Buddy, not yet," answered Beanie, determined not to let frustration get the best of him, considering the air of annoyance and irritation in the large SUV he'd rented for the family day trip to the sandbar. Much of the irritation wafted from Noelle, sitting in the passenger seat. Arms folded, she stared straight ahead, giving him somewhat of a silent treatment.

Noelle's passive-aggressiveness annoyed and irritated him, but he forced himself to stay positive and keep a good attitude, for the boys' sake, if for no other reason. His kids didn't need to witness an argument, especially when the disagreement was unwarranted. And unnecessary. At least, Beanie thought so …

And yet, he understood why his wife was upset. Truth be told, he was the cause for Noelle's ire.

He'd arrived back at the villa twelve minutes late. By that time, Noelle was in full smother mode, definitely no longer under the influence of the volcanic ash and sea kelp. When he walked into the bright, spacious kitchen empty-handed, his wife gaped at him in disbelief, which quickly turned to disappointment when he tried to explain the lack of kid-friendly fare at the grocery store.

Despite claiming to understand his predicament, Beanie had the feeling his wife blamed him for the store's luxury inventory and faulted him for not finding something the boys would snack on. He'd recounted a list of the store's products and his wife had agreed that neither Ethan nor Evan would have enjoyed those foods. But, still, she got exasperated.

"Why aren't we there yet, Daddy?"

"Because we haven't driven the number of miles we need to get to the sandbar," explained Beanie, gripping the steering wheel. "But we'll be there soon."

"Miles to the sandbar," sang Evan, clapping his hands. "Miles to the sandbar!"

"Are you sure, Daddy?" challenged Ethan. "Because that's what you said when I asked you the last time and we're still not at the sandbar. We should have been there soon by now."

"Soon by now!" Evan called out. "We're not at the sandbar!"

"Daddy, are you sure you are driving in the right direction?" asked Ethan. "Did you put the address in the GPS?"

"Daddy drive in right direction!" echoed Evan. "Daddy in the GPS!"

"Maybe we're not there because you're going the wrong way," said Ethan, his voice rising in concern.

"Ethan!" said Noelle, her sharp tone conveying her annoyance. "Get your tablet out of your backpack and play one of your games."

"But, Mommy, we have to make sure that Daddy is not—"

"Ethan, did you hear me?" Noelle twisted her body toward Ethan, to stare at him. "Daddy needs to concentrate on driving."

As Ethan mumbled his irritation, Beanie glanced at his wife, who went back to staring ahead. "I'm not having a problem concentrating."

"You don't need to be distracted by all of his questions," said Noelle. "This is our first time in the Aerie Islands. You don't know the roads. You need to pay attention."

Beanie sighed. He didn't need to know the roads to keep the road. And besides, the coastal road, a two-lane strip of concrete with lush, tropical vegetation on one side and rocks that gradually sloped down to the beach on the other, was typical of most Caribbean roads. But he had a feeling Noelle would not thank him for pointing that fact out to her.

"Mommy, can I have a banana?" asked Ethan, poking his head between the bucket seats.

"We're going to eat when we get to the sandbar," said Noelle.

"But when are we going to get to the sandbar?" whined Ethan. "When is soon?"

"Ethan, play your game, okay," said Noelle. "Mommy is not in the mood right now."

"Mommy not in mood," sang Evan. "Mommy not in mood."

"Elle, you can't still be upset about the grocery store not having kid-friendly snacks," said Beanie, glancing at his wife for a second before he focused on the road again. Ahead was a section of highway that traversed through a thick tunnel of trees, with shrubs and bushes on both sides of the road.

"I can," said Noelle, crossing her arms. "And I am."

Beanie gripped the wheel, but he wanted to throw up his hands in defeat. "But, why? It's not even a problem. We got food from the villa."

"And that food is for when we're at the villa," said Noelle. "That's why I wanted you to get snacks for the sandbar."

"There weren't any snacks at the grocery store," said Beanie, trying to keep his voice even. "I told you that. And taking food from the villa is not against the rules."

"I know it's not against the rules," snapped Noelle.

"The housekeeping staff restocks the fridge and the pantry every day with basics," said Beanie. "The villa coordinator explained that to us—"

"I remember exactly what the villa coordinator explained," snipped his wife. "I know the food will be replenished, but …"

"But?" asked Beanie, steering through trees that formed natural walls around them, blocking the sun, obscuring the blue skies and wispy white clouds of a gorgeous tropical day.

"But, what I don't understand is if there wasn't any kid-friendly food in the store then why did it take you forty minutes to figure that out?"

Beanie looked over at Noelle. "What?"

"You were gone a long time, Roland," said Noelle.

Shaking his head, Beanie said, "Elle—"

"Pay attention, Roland!" Noelle leaned forward, an edge in her voice that sent a fissure of panic through him.

"I am paying attention," he countered.

"No, you weren't," accused Noelle. "Did you see that car?"

Beanie focused on the road head. Roughly two car lengths ahead, a small sedan drove in front of him.

"That car jumped in front of you," said Noelle, accusatory.

Staring at the car's taillights, Beanie said, "Sorry, I didn't see—"

"Oh my goodness …" whispered Noelle.

Beanie shared his wife's worried sentiments. Nearly ten feet ahead, the vehicle in front of them seemed out of control, driving erratically, swerving back and forth across the road, slamming on its brakes, and then speeding up again.

"Why are they driving so crazy like that?" Noelle said.

"Crazy!" Evan clapped, giggling. "Crazy!"

"What's happening, Daddy?" asked Ethan.

"I have no idea," said Beanie, slowing his speed, trying to recall the evasive maneuvers he learned in the defensive driving class he'd taken a few years ago. "But, I'm going to—"

Noelle gasped as the vehicle did a strange 180-degree turn, tires squealing, engine roaring as the car accelerated, leaving the road, and crashed into the thicket of trees …

4

Beanie steered the SUV to the side of the road and parked on the gravelly shoulder.

"What happened, Daddy?" cried Ethan, the high pitch of his voice conveying fear and confusion. "Why are we stopping? Are we there yet?"

"Not yet, sweetie," said Noelle, reaching into her bag.

Worried about the passengers in the crashed vehicle, Beanie opened his door as he said to Noelle, "Call an ambulance."

Pulling out her phone, Noelle nodded.

"Where are you going, Daddy?" demanded Ethan, wiggling his body through the space between the front bucket seats.

"It's okay, Buddy," reassured Beanie, reaching out to ruffle Ethan's hair. "Daddy will be right back. The people in that car had an accident."

"An accident?" Ethan's eyes widened. "Are they hurt?"

"That's what Daddy is going to find out, okay, Buddy?"

"I want to go with you, Daddy."

"No, Buddy, you stay with Mommy, okay," said Beanie.

"Help Mommy make sure that Evan is okay," said Noelle. "Mommy is going to call an ambulance."

"Okay, Mommy," said Ethan, clearly not happy with his instructions as he turned to his little brother. "It's okay, Evan. Don't cry …"

Satisfied that Ethan was taking care of his big brother duties, comforting little Evan, whose lower lip quivered as he glanced about, Beanie exited the SUV. Heading around the front of the SUV to the shoulder, he jogged to the section of trees the car had crashed through. Between broken and flattened bushes, shrubs, and branches, he spotted the back of the small sedan.

Coughing from the strong stench of smoke and exhaust, Beanie approached the trunk. He peered through the back window. Frowning, he stared at the headrests of the front seats, the exploded airbags, the steering wheel, and the windshield. What he didn't see were passengers. Where was the person who'd been driving the car? Heart pounding, Beanie made his way around the side of the car, angling between the broad leaf branches. A quick check through the side windows showed an empty vehicle.

Confused, Beanie pushed away more branches as he walked to the front of the car. The vehicle had come to a stop in front of a natural barrier of stones. The large rocks sloped down, about thirty feet, to a narrow beach bordered by Seagrape trees.

Beanie spotted three people standing near one of the trees, a guy and two women. All of them wore beach apparel. The guy in board shorts and a loose-fitting t-shirt. The women, both long-haired blondes, looked similar except one wore a pink sundress, and the other had on jeans and a yellow tank top. The conversation seemed tense and from the gestures, possibly contentious. Snatches of their voices floated upwind, but the gusty breeze and the waves rolling from the sea made it impossible for Beanie to make out what they were saying.

Their body language spoke volumes, however.

The guy paced in a tight arc between the women, shaking his head and pointing accusing fingers at them. The woman in pink was more animated than the other woman, who hugged her arms around her thin frame and hung her head.

What was going on with the trio? Had they been in the car that crashed? From his vantage, which wasn't so far away, none of the group seemed injured. But then, the car didn't look so bad. The trees had absorbed the impact and suffered most of the damage. But if they had crashed their car, why would they get out and climb down to the beach? Beanie scratched his chin. Maybe they were bystanders who'd been walking along the sand and stopped to argue next to a Seagrape tree.

Giving up his pointless frustration, Beanie called out, "Hey! Hey!"

The woman in pink looked up at him.

"Did you guys have an accident?" shouted Beanie. "Are you okay?"

Instead of answering him, the woman turned to the guy, who was also looking up at Beanie. At once, something about the young guy struck Beanie as familiar. Had he seen him before? The guy and the pink sundress woman put their heads together and turned their backs to him. What was that about? Were they discussing how they were going to answer? Or maybe if they would answer? But why wouldn't they answer? It was a simple question.

"Hey!" called Beanie again, trying to temper his suspicions.

The guy glanced over his shoulder, shook his head, and yelled, "We're fine!"

"Did you have an accident?" asked Beanie again. "Is this your car?"

The woman hugging herself looked up, and yelled, "We didn't—"

The woman in pink rushed to the other woman, grabbed her arm and whispered something in her ear. As she guided the woman a few feet away from the tree, the pink sundress woman seemed to be scolding her. The woman who'd been hugging herself now used her hands to cover her face. The young guy followed the two women, caught up with them, and the three hurried along the beach, quickly increasing their distance.

We didn't … what? The girl in the yellow tank top had been going to say something. But, then the woman in pink stopped her. We didn't … have a car accident? Was that what the girl was going to say? Or was she about to shout something else? If so, what? Something the pink sundress woman didn't want her to say?

Beanie reflected on the guy in the board shorts. Why did he seem so familiar? And why, as he thought about it, did he think he'd seen the women before, as well? Still, the more important question was, what had the guy been upset about? Again, Beanie wondered what was going on with the trio.

Had they been in the crashed car? If so, why had they abandoned the vehicle? And why—

The piercing hi-low whine of sirens grabbed Beanie's attention. The ambulance. And possibly, the cops. Beanie blew out a slow breath. The police would want a statement. What would he tell them? The truth, obviously. But, should he mention the trio? They were further down the beach now. Too far away to call out to. Definitely not turning back. As the sirens grew louder, Beanie wondered if the guy and the two girls were continuing to their destination. Or running away from a bad situation.

Deciding to hold his speculations, and suspicions, at bay, Beanie turned.

Stumbling from the bramble of bushes, a young man staggered toward him.

"Help … me … please … "

The guy lurched forward, pale and sweaty, pressing a hand against the side of his head. Blood seeped between his fingers, dripping onto his cheek, rolling beneath his chin.

"What happened?" asked Beanie, his pulse ratcheting up as he hurried toward the guy.

"Hit me … " whispered the guy, dropping to his knees just as Beanie reached to help him stand.

"Hit you?" Beanie slipped an arm around the guy, struggling to hold him up. "Someone hit you? Who was it? Can you tell me what happened to you?"

"Please … help …" The guy clutched Beanie's shirt with his bloody hand and stared at him. "Please …"

As the guy's eyes fluttered and closed, a paralyzing thought struck Beanie.

He recognized the guy.

It was the lifeguard who'd been at the pool yesterday. The young, good-looking kid Carmen had accused of being a corrupting influence on her son, Marcus.

Once again, he's falling in with the wrong crowd. The pool crew. Pablo—he's the one on duty now ...

The lifeguard who'd been confronted by Fred, the guy in the cabana.

They should have fired you a long time ago! They never should have hired you! Don't deserve this job!

But, that wasn't the only thing he'd heard Fred say.

That punk needs to learn that he can't disrespect me ... he needs to be taught a lesson.

Beanie frowned. Could Fred have been talking about Pablo? It would make sense. After all—

"Sir, put your hands up ... "

Beanie glanced up.

"Now!"

Two Aerie Islands police officers pointed guns at him.

5

"Anything else you want to add?" asked the Aerie Islands detective, a trim, petite woman in a dark linen suit, who'd introduced herself as Wilhelmina Gilberto.

Detective Gilberto arrived on the scene of the car accident moments after Beanie had been marched through the crushed trees by the officers who'd ordered him to wait on the side of the road. As Noelle looked on through the windshield of the SUV, her gaze full of fear and confusion, Beanie tried his best to convey that he was okay.

His initial statement to the cops hadn't convinced them that he wasn't involved with the car crash or the assault on the lifeguard Pablo. The detective, however, was willing to give him the benefit of the doubt along with her side eye. His account of the events was corroborated by his wife, who was questioned by the officers while the detective interrogated him.

But now, the detective seemed ready to move on.

A tow truck had arrived to remove the damaged vehicle. The ambulance had sped away with Pablo strapped to a gurney, receiving emergency attention from the paramedics. There was nothing left for Detective Gilberto to do except head back to the station, Beanie supposed.

"Mr. Bean...?" asked the detective, a slight irritation in her tone. "Is there anything else you want to tell me?"

Beanie cleared his throat. "Well, actually—"

"Hey! Hey, Beanie!" shouted a voice. "Over here! Beanie!"

Another voice he recognized, thought Beanie as he turned to the right.

A blast from the not-too-distant past jogged across the street toward him.

Joshua Howard, thought Beanie. His red hair flopping, catching the rays of the mid-morning sun, Beanie's former intern smiled brightly. Despite the young guy's genial disposition, Beanie couldn't help remembering the harrowing situation he and Joshua had found themselves in while investigating a murder.

"Mr. Bean, if there's nothing else," said the detective, angling away from him.

Sighing, Beanie shook his head. "No, there's nothing else."

Detective Gilberto turned and strode away as Joshua reached him.

"Beanie, man, what are you doing here?" Laughing, Joshua grabbed him in a bear hug. "Good to see you, man!"

"You, too ..." said Beanie, extracting himself from the gregarious young guy with a few good-natured claps on his back. "How are you?"

Beanie and Joshua walked closer to Beanie's rented SUV.

"Oh, man, doing great," said Joshua, nodding.

"In the Aerie Islands?" asked Beanie, glancing straight ahead at the SUV. Still in the car, Noelle shook her head, giving him a quizzical look. Beanie held up a finger, gesturing for her to give him a minute. "When did you move? And what happened to the podcast you were working on?"

Joshua looked away, then glanced down before sighing. With a shrug and a sheepish look, he said, "The podcast didn't work out. Turns out, the Fury is a very popular subject."

"Unfortunately, he is ..." said Beanie, forcing himself not to shudder as he thought about the heinous cannibal who'd terrorized the Palmchat Islands for decades before he was apprehended.

"There are hundreds of podcasts about the Fury," said Joshua.

"Almost as many as there are for Manson, Bundy, and Dahmer. It was way too much competition … anyway, I decided to apply for a job here in the Aerie Islands at the *Aerie Islands Observer*… and I got the gig!"

"Good for you," said Beanie, glancing toward the SUV again. Noelle was frowning, not surprisingly.

"Actually, I started two weeks ago," said Joshua. "This is going to be my first story."

"I'm sure you'll do great," said Beanie, thankful he didn't have to cover the lifeguard's assault. If he were back home in St. Killian, and not on vacation, he'd probably be trying to get statements from detectives, officers, eyewitnesses, and—

Thinking of eyewitnesses, Beanie recalled the odd trio on the beach. The guy, the girl in the pink sundress, and the woman wearing jeans and a yellow tank top. Had they seen the car accident? Did they know anything about the assault on Pablo? Were they eyewitnesses? Or—

"… nice to have your help …"

Shaken from his thoughts, Beanie stared at Joshua. The former intern looked hopeful but worried.

"Sorry … what did you say?"

Joshua said, "I really need to do a good job on this story. So, I was hoping …"

"Hoping?" asked Beanie, though he wasn't sure he wanted to know.

"Well … " Joshua sighed. "I was hoping you'll be my mentor again and help me investigate the story."

6

"Roland, we are on vacation," said Noelle, striding across the spacious master bedroom.

Beanie lounged on the king-sized bed, unwinding after a long day at the popular sandbar they'd finally arrived at, following the vehicle crash. They'd lost an hour and a half because of the detour but the boys still had a great time. Beanie was just happy that Ethan and Evan hadn't been traumatized by the accident. He was even more ecstatic about the plethora of food stalls on the sandbar.

"I know we're on vacation, Elle," said Beanie, crossing his ankles as he took in his surroundings. The room, which seemed almost as big as their modest home back in St. Killian, featured luxurious furnishings in mango, mahogany, and teak wood. Natural-fiber sisal rugs covered the bamboo floors. Beyond the plantation shutters that framed a row of French doors, the sun was setting on a glorious day.

"Do you?" challenged Noelle. "Are you sure you understand what 'we are on vacation' means? Because I don't think you do. Because if you did, you would not have agreed to help Joshua Howard write a story!"

Beanie sighed. "Babe—"

"No, don't 'babe' me, okay," Noelle told him stomping toward the massive bamboo wood wardrobe. "You are not supposed to be working. You are supposed to be relaxing."

"I'm not going to be working," said Beanie. "I'm going to be giving direction and advice."

His wife opened the wardrobe. "And while you're giving direction and advice, what will the boys and I be doing?"

"This direction and advice will not interfere with our vacation," promised Beanie. "And, actually, I've already sent Joshua in the right direction, which is to the police station to get a statement from the cops. After that, he's headed to the hospital to talk to the victim. With that information, Joshua can write his story. When you think about it, my work is done."

Noelle gave him a half smile, though her gaze was still skeptical. "I hope so. The boys are looking forward to going to the zoo tomorrow."

"So am I," said Beanie as Noelle turned and headed under a wide archway that led to the master bathroom.

The Aerie Islands Zoo was famous for its collection of snakes, many of which had belonged to an eccentric billionaire who'd donated them to the zoo along with a sizable trust to fund the facility. Among the exotic reptiles was a family of African Black Mambas, a popular tourist attraction.

Sighing, Beanie settled back against the pillows, which were filled with goose feathers. Certainly a lot fancier than the cotton he slept on at home. As he closed his eyes, Beanie warned himself not to get used to the luxury as his thoughts drifted to Joshua Howard.

After encountering Chuck and Flo, he hadn't expected to see another familiar face. Joshua was only slightly less intrusive than the wealthy ex-pats. And Beanie was happy to help the guy. After all, he'd mentored Joshua before, when the spunky redhead was an intern at the *Palmchat Gazette*. Beanie was interested in observing how much, if any, of his tutelage had remained. Not that Beanie would take any credit for Joshua's success, but … it would be nice to know that his investment hadn't been in vain.

Beanie was certain Joshua could write a good, engaging story with details from the cops and the victim, Pablo. Thinking about the hunky, young lifeguard brought to Beanie's mind the incident at the pool. Fred, whose last name Beanie didn't know, had accused Pablo of being lazy. He'd threatened to report Pablo for slacking off and had tried to assault the young man.

"Help ... me ... "

An image of Pablo, staggering, holding the back of his head as blood streamed down his fingers.

Beanie's eyes opened.

Pablo had been assaulted. Likely hit in the back of the head.

Could Fred have done that?

After all, Beanie had overheard Fred and the store clerk talking. *That punk needs to learn that he can't disrespect me. He needs to be taught a lesson. The guy I know has ties to the PC-5 ...*

Could the punk have been Pablo? Could Fred have arranged for Pablo to be assaulted? By some thug with ties to the PC-5? Beanie wasn't sure. But he wondered if maybe he should have told the detective about Fred and the store clerk. And about the incident with Pablo and Fred at the pool. Maybe—

Beanie's phone chirped.

A text message.

Swinging his legs over the side of the bed, Beanie grabbed his phone from the nightstand. He swiped his thumb across the screen, accessed the message, and read it.

JOSHUA HOWARD
Hey, it's Joshua. Could we meet up tomorrow?
Case took a wild turn and I could use ur advice.

Frowning, Beanie replied.

what kind of turn?

victim, Pablo Lima, died two hours ago. Cops
say he was murdered.

7

"Are you serious?" Noelle slammed the door of the sub-Zero refrigerator and turned to glare at Beanie. "You're going to meet with Joshua about a murder case?"

Beanie stared at his lovely wife, wary of the irritation in her gaze. Clearing his throat, he said, "He just needs some advice on how to construct the article and conduct his investigation."

"Shouldn't he already know how to do that?" demanded Noelle, arms folded across her chest. "Didn't you teach him? He was your intern, right?"

Sighing, Beanie rubbed his eyes and then propped an elbow on the large island where he sat in the equally large kitchen. Afternoon sunlight floated through the windows, casting a golden glow across the room, giving the space a cozy, comfortable warmth.

His wife's cold demeanor was disappointing, considering how well the day had turned out, thus far.

The morning began with a hearty breakfast. Then they'd piled into the SUV for their trip to the Aerie Islands zoo. The boys were thrilled and delighted by turtles, bats, hundreds of species of birds, reptiles, and butterflies. The House of Snakes exhibit, not surprisingly, had been their favorite. When the trip was over, as Beanie drove back to the villa,

Ethan and Evan talked non-stop about the Black Mamba family. They'd gotten tickets to a special event that allowed them to see a live milking of the snake's venom, which would be used to make antivenom that would be shipped to countries in Africa.

Following the zoo, they'd had lunch and then returned to the villa. Beanie and the boys went to the pool while Noelle had another treatment, one Beanie had hoped would relax her and alter her mood like the seaweed scrub. She'd returned to announce she planned to sleep while the boys were at the Children's center before they all went to dinner at eight, which was three hours later.

"Roland …"

Bristling at the sharp rebuke in his wife's tone, Beanie said, "Yes, Joshua was my intern. I mentored him. And that's probably why I feel a bit invested in his career. I want him to do well. God knows I could have used some help when I started out. Instead, I had to deal with Caleb Olivier, a crabby old guy with declining skills who saw me as a threat to his job."

"Look, I get that you want Joshua to do well," said Noelle. "But we are on vacation. I don't want you to get distracted by some murder mystery."

"I won't," promised Beanie, detecting less annoyance in his wife's tone. "I'm going to meet him at the *Aerie Observer* and give him some direction. That's all. I'll be back in time for dinner."

"You better be," warned Noelle, shaking her head as she pivoted and left the kitchen.

An hour later at the *Aerie Observer*, Beanie sat across from Joshua in the former intern's cubicle, which was significantly more spacious than Beanie's tiny cube at the *Palmchat Gazette*.

"So, tell me what you found out from the police," requested Beanie.

Leaning back in his chair, Joshua said, "First of all, the victim, Pablo Lima, a twenty-two-year-old Aerie Islands resident, born and raised here, died from his injuries."

"Which were?" asked Beanie, recalling the blood seeping down the side of the lifeguard's face. "Why do the police think he was murdered?"

"Well, first they thought he'd died because of the injuries he'd sustained in the car crash," said Joshua, consulting notes on his phone.

Scratching his chin, Beanie asked, "The police think there's a connection between Pablo's death and the car crash? Do they think he was in that car?"

"They do," answered Joshua.

"You spoke with an officer?" asked Beanie, making sure.

"Well, I have a source at the police department."

Curious about the slightly smug smile on the former intern's face, Beanie said, "Always good to have."

"It's Friday. Remember her?" asked Joshua, beaming with pride. "My girlfriend."

"How could I forget Friday?" asked Beanie, nodding as an image of the young woman filled his mind.

"Anyway, she works as an administrative assistant for the Chief of Detectives," explained Joshua. "Friday told me that Detective Gilberto thought Pablo Lima might have been thrown from the car and hit his head on a tree. But then the medical examiner ruled it out. Said Lima's injuries weren't consistent with being thrown from a car or being hit in the head."

"So how did he die?"

"The M.E. said he was poisoned," said Joshua.

"Poisoned?"

"Crazy, huh?"

Beanie asked, "What kind of poison?"

"The cops are not sure yet," said Joshua. "But they're working on it. And Friday thinks they might be able to tell if Lima was poisoned before or after he was in the accident."

"So, he was definitely in the car when it crashed?"

"One of his shoes was found inside the vehicle, which puts him in the car."

"Interesting ..." remarked Beanie, scratching his chin.

"You want to know what's really interesting?" asked Joshua. "It wasn't even Pablo's car."

"It wasn't?"

Shaking his head, Joshua said, "It was registered to a … let's see, I got the name here … Sasha Hidalgo. She works at the Aerie Islands Zoo but she used to work at the place where you and your family are staying. Aerie Islands Spa Club."

"Was she in the accident with Pablo?"

"Sasha Hidalgo told the cops that Pablo borrowed her car," said Joshua, reading from his phone. "She says he didn't tell her where he was going. Friday was thinking he went to hook up with this girl named Daisy Cox because her purse, with her wallet and ID, was also found in the car."

"So, Ms. Cox was also in the accident?"

"Daisy Cox claims she wasn't," said Joshua. "She told the police she must have accidentally left her purse in the car, which Detective Gilberto didn't really believe, according to Friday."

Beanie frowned. "Does seem unlikely."

"However, someone was in the car with him, because the cops found female hair in the backseat," said Joshua.

"Who'd they belong to?"

"Cops don't know yet," said Joshua. "Anyway, now I'm wondering what to do next. My story is coming out tomorrow but it's kind of … uneventful. Just the who, what, when, where, and why, you know?"

"The basic facts are important," said Beanie. "You use them as the foundation for any future stories or follow-ups."

"Yeah, I know," said Joshua, placing his phone on the desk. "I just wish I could have gotten a statement from Pablo. He never regained consciousness so the cops couldn't get a statement from him. And from the statement you gave the cops, he didn't say much of anything to you, either."

Beanie nodded. "He just asked for help."

"Did he seem like he'd been poisoned?" asked Joshua. "Was he foaming at the mouth, or anything?"

Beanie said, "Just thought he had a head injury. He collapsed and I thought it was from loss of blood, but maybe it was the poison in his system."

Fred, the guy who'd confronted Pablo Lima and told the store clerk he wanted to teach the punk a lesson, came to Beanie's mind. Last night, he'd wondered if Fred could have been behind Pablo's assault. Could the store clerk's PC-5 contact have attacked Lima? Now, Beanie wondered if Fred could have arranged for Pablo Lima to be poisoned.

Beanie wasn't sure.

The island cartel wasn't known for poisoning people, but it was possible, Beanie supposed.

"So, what should I do next?"

"I would talk to both Sasha Hidalgo and Daisy Cox," said Beanie. "I know they gave statements to the police but sometimes witnesses are more relaxed around reporters."

Nodding, Joshua said, "Good idea. Would you mind coming with me? To talk to Sasha Hidalgo and Daisy Cox? That is, if they'll agree to talk to me."

"Sure," agreed Beanie, chuckling at Joshua's relieved expression. "But not tonight. I've got dinner with my family and if I'm late, my wife will kill me."

8

"We lied to the cops," announced Daisy Cox, arms wrapped around her torso as she paced back and forth across the living area of the small apartment she shared with her best friend, Sasha Hidalgo.

Beanie and Joshua, who'd secured Daisy Cox's address from his girlfriend Friday, had arrived at the eight-unit complex on the west side of the island early that morning. With Noelle scheduled for yoga and more body treatments, Beanie dropped the boys off at the Children's center where they had a schedule of activities that would keep them busy for the next few hours.

After picking up Joshua from the *Aerie Observer*, Beanie and the former intern stopped for coffee and then continued to Daisy Cox's residence. On the way, Joshua imparted additional information he'd learned from Friday the previous night.

"Apparently, the police recovered a bottle of top-shelf scotch beneath the seat of the car involved in the accident," said Joshua, consulting his phone. "There were fingerprints on the bottle. One set belonged to Pablo Lima. The other prints belonged to a guy named Marcus Taylor."

"Marcus Taylor?" asked Beanie, taking a quick look at Joshua. "Are you sure?"

"Yeah," said the former intern. "Why?"

"I know him," said Beanie. "Well, I don't mean I personally know him, but I know of him. I know his mother. She's friends with my wife. Marcus is a lifeguard at the Aerie Islands Spa Club."

"Yeah, that's in my notes," said Joshua. "And the other prints in the car belonged to Sasha Hidalgo and Daisy Cox. Detective Gilberto questioned them again, and both girls came clean about being in the car that day. They gave up Marcus, and when he was questioned, he didn't deny being in the car."

"So, Sasha, Daisy, and Marcus were in the car with Pablo when it crashed?"

Joshua nodded. "Right. They told the cops that Pablo got sick, lost control of the car, and crashed. Then Sasha, Daisy, and Marcus got out of the car to go and find help."

Thinking of the trio on the beach, Beanie wondered if those three had been the other passengers in the wrecked vehicle. Hadn't he thought the guy seemed familiar? Had he been looking at Marcus Taylor? Was Daisy Cox one of the girls who'd been with the guy?

Beanie's question had been answered when Daisy Cox answered the door.

As soon as he saw the petite woman with large doe eyes, a small nose, and a Cupid's bow mouth, he recalled her as the timid girl he'd seen down on the beach after the car accident that had delayed his family's trip to the sandbar.

"You lied to the cops?" echoed Joshua.

Daisy's admission, which she'd blurted out as soon as Joshua asked his first question, was surprising.

Even more shocking was the realization that Beanie knew the young woman.

"Who is we?" asked Joshua.

"Me, Sasha, and Marcus," said Daisy, head lowered, soft buttery tresses hanging like a curtain around her head, obscuring her freckled face.

"What lie did you tell?" Beanie asked.

Sighing, Daisy said, "That Pablo got sick and crashed the car."

Joshua asked, "So Pablo didn't get sick and crash the car?"

Exhaling, Daisy shook her head.

"Why did you lie to the police?" asked Joshua.

"I didn't want to," insisted Daisy. "I got overruled by Sasha and Marcus. Before Pablo died, we were going to just stay quiet and not tell anyone we'd been in the car with him. And it might have worked, but then the cops found my purse in the car, which I forgot. And I had to give them some idiot story about not remembering that I had accidentally left my purse in the car, which was ridiculous. Which I told Sasha and Marcus. I told them the police wouldn't believe me, but they told me to stay quiet and stick to the story."

Beanie asked, "So what really happened?"

Groaning, Daisy stopped pacing and dropped her face in her hands. "We'd been drinking. A lot. And then Marcus and Pablo got into an argument about something. I don't even remember what. Then Marcus and Pablo started fighting. Me and Sasha were yelling at them to stop. Then Marcus started hitting Pablo. And that made Pablo lose control of the car and then he crashed into the trees. Then we all got out of the car. Pablo was beyond angry at Marcus and he lunged at him. They started fighting again. Pablo grabbed Marcus and wrestled him to the ground. Me and Sasha got scared and we ran down to the beach. Then, like, fifteen minutes later, Marcus climbed down the rocks and joined us. Sasha was like, where is Pablo? Marcus said he didn't know, but we needed to leave."

"I think I saw the three of you on the beach," admitted Beanie.

Gaping at him, Daisy asked, "That was you?"

"I yelled down to you," said Beanie. "Asked if you had been in the accident?"

"I was going to yell back that we had, but we were okay," said Daisy. "But Sasha told me to stay quiet. Then Marcus said we needed to leave. I didn't want to go. But Sasha said you had probably called the cops and they would find the liquor in her car and we'd be charged with drinking and driving."

"But you weren't driving," said Joshua.

"I realize that," said Daisy, resuming her manic pacing. "But at the time, I was freaking out. I was thinking the cops would find some way to blame all of us for the accident and I would lose my job."

"So the three of you decided to pretend you'd never been in the car with Pablo," said Beanie.

Daisy nodded. "But then the cops found my purse in the car. Once that happened, I knew it was only a matter of time before they figured out that we were in the car. And, of course, they did. So Marcus came up with another lie for us to tell."

"Pablo got sick, lost control, and crashed," said Beanie.

"I know I shouldn't have gone along with them. Should have been honest. But after Pablo died, they said we would get in trouble," Daisy said. "Marcus said we could be charged with involuntary manslaughter, or something, even though neither me nor Sasha was driving."

"So are you going to be honest with the police?" asked Joshua.

"Going to the cops won't matter if the others won't tell the truth," said Daisy, walking to the loveseat and dropping down onto the thin cushion.

Beanie said, "Ms. Cox, it's very unlikely that you or your friends will be charged with involuntary manslaughter."

Daisy looked up at him. "You don't know that."

"Pablo didn't die because of the car crash," said Joshua.

"What?" Daisy stared at them, eyes wide. "He didn't?"

"After the car crashed, you, Pablo, Marcus, and Sasha got out of the vehicle, right?"

Sighing, Daisy said, "I know that, but … Marcus said the cops—"

"Marcus probably doesn't want you to go to the police because he's probably responsible for Pablo's death," said Joshua.

Daisy's eyes widened. "You think Marcus killed Pablo?"

"We don't know who killed Pablo," said Beanie, giving Joshua a quick glance, hoping his former intern would refrain from casting blame. They didn't have enough information to speculate about suspects yet. "Joshua is just trying to get information for his article, as he explained to you."

"Well, I know Marcus wouldn't kill Pablo," said Daisy. "They were friends. I mean, okay, yeah they were fighting in the car, but it was about something stupid."

"What were they fighting about?"

Looking away, Daisy shrugged. "I don't know. I mean … I'm sure it was something dumb. Guys get mad at each other all the time and they get over it. Marcus would not have killed Pablo. I don't believe that."

"And yet Pablo is dead," said Joshua.

"Are you saying Marcus beat Pablo to death?" asked Daisy, her face shrouded in doubt.

Beanie said, "Pablo was poisoned."

Daisy's doubt turned to disbelief. "Poisoned? What? How?"

"The police don't know yet," said Joshua.

"Then I know for sure Marcus didn't kill Pablo," said Daisy. "Where would Marcus get poison?"

"Depends on what kind of poison killed Pablo," said Joshua. "If it was roach poison, or rat poison, then—"

The hollow sound of a jaunty samba song cut through the air, interrupting Joshua.

"Just a second." Daisy jumped up and crossed the room to the galley kitchen. "My phone."

As Daisy took the phone call, Beanie took a moment to reflect on her story. Four kids in a car. Drinking. A fight breaks out. The car crashes. Three of the passengers take off in a panic, fearful of repercussions. One is left behind to die. The only thing that didn't make sense was Pablo's death. How had the young lifeguard been poisoned? Who had poisoned him? And why?

"Sorry, I have to get ready for work," said Daisy, her tone apologetic. "My boss needs me to cover a shift and I need the extra money, so …"

"No worries," said Joshua. "Thanks for talking to me."

"Wait. You're not going to put what I told you in the paper, are you?" asked Daisy, her expression stricken. "About Marcus and Pablo fighting? Because you can't! The cops will know I lied. I promised Marcus and Sasha I would stick to the story we told the police!"

"If you wanted to speak off the record, you should have told me," said Joshua, frowning

"If you write about Marcus and Pablo fighting in your article, I'll deny it," warned Daisy, her fear turning into a fierce scowl. "I'll accuse you of publishing fake news."

Scoffing, Joshua said, "Are you serious?"

"You don't have any proof of what I told you," said Daisy.

"Mr. Bean can corroborate my story," said Joshua. "He heard you say—"

"Why don't we let Ms. Cox get ready for work," suggested Beanie, hoping to de-escalate the situation.

Joshua gave him a confused, reluctant look. "But—"

"And, Ms. Cox, if you'd rather not to quoted in the article," said Beanie, "then I'm sure Mr. Howard can accommodate your wishes."

9

"So if I can't quote Daisy Cox in my story," began Joshua, buckling himself into the passenger seat of the SUV. "Then how do I tell my readers what she said? It's kind of explosive information. don't you think?"

"Witnesses lying to the cops," said Beanie, starting the ignition. "Unfortunately, it happens all the time. Which doesn't make it any less explosive. It's great information."

"And I can't even put it in my article," grumbled Joshua.

"Actually, you can," said Beanie, scrolling through the dashboard GPS for their next location, which was already programmed into the device—the Aerie Islands Zoo. Sasha Hidalgo, the next witness Joshua planned to interview, worked at the facility. According to Joshua's research, Sasha was an intern to the zoo's Assistant Herpetologist.

"How?" Joshua threw up his hands. "If I tell her story, she's gonna say it's fake news. Probably leave a bunch of negative comments on my social media channels accusing me of unethical journalism. Can't get that kind of reputation."

"Instead of a direct witness involved in the event," said Beanie, glancing at the SUV's backup camera display as he reversed out of the parking space. "Daisy Cox becomes an anonymous source with knowledge of the incident who agreed to speak on the condition of anonymity."

"Oh …" said Joshua, nodding. "Yeah, I could do that."

"And the anonymous source alleges that the victim and another passenger in the car had a physical altercation, which caused the crash," said Beanie. "That allegation disputes what the vehicle's passengers told the police."

"That's perfect," said Joshua, making notes on his phone.

Steering the SUV onto the main road, Beanie asked, "So what did you think of Daisy Cox's story?"

"Not sure what to think," admitted Joshua. "I mean, it's not implausible. She and her friends are drinking and fighting in a car, which ends up in a crash. Then the two guys continue the fight outside the car. She and her friend take off. The other guy, Marcus, takes off with the girls. The three of them come up with a ridiculous lie. I can see that happening, but …"

"But …?" prompted Beanie, keeping an eye on the GPS instructions as he drove along the same coastal road where the accident involving Daisy, Sasha, Marcus, and Pablo had occurred.

"But the weird thing is that Pablo was poisoned," said Joshua. "Feels like it has nothing to do with the car crash or the fight with Marcus."

"I was thinking the same thing," said Beanie, recalling his fleeting suspicions of Fred, the man who'd confronted Pablo at the Aerie Islands Spa Club pool and later asked the store clerk for help in teaching an unnamed punk a lesson.

"And then I think," said Joshua. "Why would any of them lie to the police if they weren't responsible for Pablo's death? I get that they were scared and panicked, but the car crash didn't kill Pablo. He was poisoned."

Remembering Daisy's wide-eyed shock, Beanie said, "But they didn't know that."

"Unless they did," said Joshua. "Well, not Daisy and Sasha. But … what if Marcus knew?"

"You suspect Marcus?" asked Beanie, interested in the direction of the former intern's thoughts and speculation.

"Daisy said Marcus and Pablo got out of the car and kept fighting," said Joshua, "then she and Sasha took off. Marcus joined them later. So, there's a period of time when Daisy and Sasha don't know what's going on with Marcus and Pablo."

"You think Marcus killed Pablo before he joined Sasha and Daisy?" asked Beanie, signaling to switch lanes as he approached the ramp leading off the highway.

"I don't know," admitted Joshua. "If Pablo had died from some sort of head trauma, I would say yes. But, do I think Marcus poisoned Pablo?"

"Possible, but not really probable."

"Right," agreed Joshua. "Poisoning someone is like, sly and sneaky. It's not violent. Marcus and Pablo were in a combative moment. How do you poison a guy in that type of situation?"

"Well, you know, there are lots of different poisons," said Beanie as he turned left onto the two-lane road that would take them to the Aerie Islands Zoo. "And different ways to poison people. It's not always slipping something into someone's drink. A few years ago, when he was working undercover, Leo Bronson was chloroformed by someone who sprayed the anesthetic in his face."

"Are you serious?" Joshua shook his head. "I never knew that. What happened?"

"I'll tell you the story on the way back to the *Aerie Observer*," promised Beanie. "But, my point is, you could spray poison in someone's face. You could inject someone with poison."

"Yeah, you're right," said Joshua. "Like that case from decades ago where an assassin killed a guy by poking him with an umbrella that had ricin in the tip."

Beanie nodded as he turned into the zoo's entrance, driving past the large stone pedestal sign displaying the facility's official name: AERIE ISLANDS ZOOLOGICAL GARDEN CENTER.

"So, how do you think I should approach Sasha?" asked Joshua.

Heading toward the parking lot, Beanie said, "Let's just start by asking her for an account of what happened. We'll see what she says and go from there ..."

Thirty minutes later, after several passes around the parking lot before securing a spot, Beanie stood with Joshua inside the large, but cramped office of the Assistant Herpetologist.

Leaning on the edge of a huge mahogany desk littered with documents, books, and a few empty food receptacles was Sasha Hidalgo.

Beanie was not surprised to recognize her as the girl in the pink sundress he'd seen arguing with Marcus near the Seagrape tree after the car accident.

He was also not shocked by her scowl and defensive attitude.

Dressed in a white lab coat, she was a pretty girl with creamy medium tan skin, but the blonde hair, obviously not natural, didn't quite work with her Mediterranean complexion. Nevertheless, she had the sultry confidence to pull it off.

"Is this going to take all day?" demanded Sasha. "Because I only have twenty minutes left on my break, and—"

"No, it won't take too long," assured Joshua. "Thank you for talking to me."

"So what do you want to ask me?" Sasha asked, crossing her arms over her chest. "I told the cops everything I know. You can ask them."

"Can you tell us what happened that day?" asked Joshua. "In your own words."

With an exaggerated exhale, Sasha Hidalgo said, "Pablo got sick, lost control of the car, and crashed it. Then me, Marcus, and Daisy went to get help."

"Did you find help?" asked Beanie, glancing around the office. Among the framed degrees on the pale gray walls were several smaller certificates and a few licenses. A tall credenza behind the desk housed more books, more documents, files bulging the papers, and a dozen, or so 3 x 5 photographs of a slight, bespeckled man smiling as he held up different types of snakes. The Assistant Herpetologist, Beanie assumed.

"Yeah, I think Marcus did," said Sasha. "But, getting help didn't matter because Pablo died, so ..."

"None of you had phones?" asked Joshua.

Beanie glanced at the girl, waiting for her response. Sasha Hidalgo looked perturbed, and she glanced away as she said, "I don't remember, listen—"

"Why did you initially lie to the cops?" asked Joshua. "You said you weren't in the car, but—"

"I panicked, okay?" Sasha shrugged and flipped a swath of blonde hair over her shoulder. "Look—"

"Was Pablo drinking?" asked Joshua.

Sasha frowned. "Drinking?"

"Is that why he got sick?" Joshua asked. "Because he was drunk?"

Rolling her eyes, Sasha said, "I don't know. And I don't have anything else to say to you, okay?"

"Were Pablo and Marcus fighting in the car?" asked Joshua.

"Fighting?" asked Sasha, looking disgusted. "Why would you think that?"

Joshua said. "Daisy Cox told me that—"

"Daisy is a liar," said Sasha. "And I need to get back to work. We're milking today."

"Milking?" asked Beanie, curious.

"We're milking venom from a black mamba," said Sasha. "Now, I have to leave and you need to go."

Back in the SUV, Joshua frowned as he buckled his seatbelt. "Well, I botched that."

Turning the ignition over, Beanie said, "I don't think so."

"She didn't give me anything," said Joshua. "Maybe I should have used a different technique to question her."

"I think the rapid-fire questions were good," said Beanie, backing out of the parking space, carefully maneuvering between the two cars waiting to fight over it. "They can trip people up and then they slip up and tell you something they meant to keep to themselves. It's hard to think of a quick answer, especially when you're trying to lie."

"Sasha didn't seem to get tripped up."

"She relied on a supposedly faulty memory and lack of knowledge," said Beanie.

Scoffing, Joshua said, "I don't remember and I don't know."

"That's what witnesses will say when they don't want to tell the truth," said Beanie, navigating through the traffic jam in the parking lot.

"I thought she was lying, too," said Joshua. "But, how do I prove it."

"It's not your job to prove it," cautioned Beanie. "It's your job to report it to the public."

"Yeah, I know," said Joshua. "But it would be dope to solve murders like you do."

"Not so sure how dope it is," said Beanie, chuckling as he drove away from the zoo grounds. "Dangerous, for sure. But helping to put the bad guys behind bars can be rewarding."

"Speaking of bad guys," said Joshua. "We only have one more person to talk to—Marcus."

10

"I told the cops what happened," mumbled Marcus, sitting at the round table in the breakfast nook, elbows propped on the surface.

Ten minutes ago, Beanie and Joshua had arrived in Starfish Cove, a settlement on the island's north coast. Populated with small, modest homes, palm trees, and well-maintained lawns, the area reminded Beanie of his neighborhood in Oyster Farms.

Marcus greeted them at the door dressed in board shorts with bleary eyes and a laconic expression. He'd been asleep on the couch when Joshua rang the doorbell, which was why it had taken him several minutes to answer. After inviting Beanie and Joshua to a seat, Marcus dropped down into a chair and stared at them, reminding Beanie of a goat dreaming of sweet grass.

"I know you spoke to the police," said Joshua. "But, for my story, I'd like to get a direct quote, if you don't mind."

Sitting across from Marcus, and to the right of Joshua, Beanie observed Carmen's son. Up close, he looked even more like his mother, but he didn't share her vigor or attentiveness.

Rubbing his eyes, Marcus said, "Pablo got sick and crashed the car."

"Then you, Sasha, and Daisy went to look for help?" asked Joshua.

Marcus nodded.

"None of you had phones to call for help?"

"Guess we didn't think to use them," said Marcus, shrugging as he leaned back in his chair. "I don't know. Guess we panicked."

"Why did you panic?" asked Beanie.

Marcus sighed. "We'd all been drinking. Didn't want to get in trouble."

"Only the driver would have gotten ticketed for drinking while driving," said Joshua. "So, if you weren't driving then—"

"I said we panicked," said Marcus, giving Joshua a dirty look. "We were drunk, okay? Not thinking straight."

Nodding, Joshua asked, "So, were you and Pablo friends?"

Marcus scowled, then rubbed his eyes, looking away. "Yeah, we were cool."

"No problems or issues between you two?" asked Joshua.

Observing the former intern, Beanie had a feeling about where he was heading with the line of questioning. And he was impressed.

Marcus frowned. "Problems between us?"

"No beef or anything?" pressed Joshua.

"Why you asking me that?" asked Marcus, glaring at Joshua.

Joshua said, "I was wondering because you and Pablo were fighting in the car before it crashed, and—"

"Wait, what?" Marcus sat forward. "Fighting in the car? Who said we were fighting in the car?"

"Were you?" asked Joshua.

"Who told you that?" Marcus demanded.

"Daisy Cox," said Joshua.

"Daisy?" Marcus cursed under his breath. "When did you talk to her? Is she trying to blame the car accident on me? Did she tell you it was my fault that Pablo crashed the car?"

Joshua said, "Daisy said you and Pablo were fighting and you punched him and he lost control of the car. After the crash, the two of you got out of the car, and continued the fight."

Shaking his head, Marcus cursed Daisy again. "Stupid girl can't keep her mouth shut for nothing."

"Is it true?" asked Joshua. "Were you and Pablo fighting in the car that day?"

Beanie said, "Daisy told us that she and Sasha went down to the beach when you and Pablo fought outside the car. Then you joined them several minutes later. What happened between the time when you fought with Pablo and when you went down to the beach?"

Marcus shook his head. "What do you mean?"

Joshua asked, "Was Pablo still alive when you left the accident scene and went down to the beach?"

"You keep your mouth shut!"

The harsh command shot through the air like a cannon, causing Beanie to jump slightly as he glanced at Joshua, who also seemed spooked.

"Do not say another word, Marcus!"

Recognizing the voice, Beanie angled in his chair to look over his shoulder.

Carmen Taylor yanked her purse from her arm and threw it onto the couch as she stomped toward the breakfast nook.

"What are you doing questioning my son?" demanded Carmen, scowling at Beanie, nostrils flaring.

Joshua said, "Ma'am, my name is Joshua Howard. I work for the *Aerie Observer* and I wanted to ask Marcus a few questions about the death of Pablo—"

"I don't want you talking to my son," warned Carmen, glaring at Joshua. "You're not the cops. He doesn't have to answer your questions."

Hoping to deescalate the situation, Beanie said, "Joshua just wanted to get Marcus' side of the story—"

"You think because Noelle and I are friends that you can come into my home and accuse my son of something that was not his fault?" Carmen screeched.

Hands up, Beanie said, "No, not at all. Joshua is just doing his due diligence by talking to all parties involved—"

"Marcus is not involved with Pablo's death!" Carmen insisted. "He already talked to the cops and he doesn't have anything else to say, especially not to some reporter who'll twist his words and try to make him look guilty!"

"I wouldn't do that," said Joshua. "I'm only interested in the facts."

"I'm only interested in the both of you getting out of my house," said Carmen. "Now! And don't come back!"

11

"That went well," grumbled Joshua as he slammed the passenger door and buckled his seatbelt.

Not surprised by the former intern's glum tone, Beanie said, "Don't get discouraged, okay? Witnesses aren't always cooperative. They don't have to answer our questions."

"Yeah, I know," said Joshua, slouching in the bucket seat.

"But, look at it like this," said Beanie, starting the SUV. "You spoke to the three other passengers who were in the car accident. You've got good information for your story."

"But I don't have proof that Marcus killed Pablo," said Joshua.

Beanie shifted into drive and steered away from the curb. "That's what you think happened?"

Nodding, Joshua said, "First of all, Daisy Cox said Marcus and Pablo were fighting, and I believe her. Sasha Hidalgo was way too quick to claim that Daisy was lying. And Marcus didn't outright deny the fight. He said Daisy couldn't keep her mouth shut. Makes me think Marcus told Daisy to stay quiet about the fight."

"That's possible."

"And then there's that period of time when Daisy and Sasha went down to the beach, but Marcus was still fighting with Pablo," said Joshua. "And then Marcus joins Daisy and Sasha on the beach."

"That's when I saw the three of them," said Beanie, driving through the neighborhood.

"So what happened during the fight between Marcus and Pablo after they got out of the car?" asked Joshua. "Daisy and Sasha weren't around to know. Did Marcus poison Pablo during that window of time? Did he spray something in Pablo's face? Like what you told me happened to Leo Bronson? Something that ended up killing Pablo?"

Beanie gripped the steering wheel. "When I saw Pablo, before he collapsed, he was stumbling and bleeding from a head wound."

"Marcus could have sprayed some type of poison that momentarily blinded Pablo," suggested Joshua. "And then Pablo might have fallen or walked into a tree."

"It's possible," allowed Beanie.

"But you don't think so?"

"Normally, before I speculate about any possible suspects," said Beanie, "I like to do a little motive, means, opportunity test."

Joshua said, "I'm down for that. Let's start with Daisy. I'd definitely say she had opportunity because she was in the car with Pablo the day he was poisoned."

"But what about means? Motive?"

"She could have had means," said Joshua. "Especially if Pablo was poisoned with something sprayed in his face. But motive? Not sure. I'd have to do more investigation about their relationship. Ask her more questions. Talk to other people who knew them."

"I'd say Sasha Hidalgo had opportunity and possibly means," said Beanie. "As for motive, it's the same situation as with Daisy. You'd need to do more investigation."

"That leaves us with Marcus," said Joshua. "I'd say he's got opportunity, means, and motive. He was fighting with Pablo in the car. There was some kind of beef. Wouldn't be hard to find out. I could talk to some of the other employees at the Aerie Islands Spa Club. People like to gossip about their coworkers."

Beanie said, "What you need is more details about the poisoning.

How was Pablo poisoned? What kind of poison was it? Because the truth is, maybe Pablo got food poisoning. Sometimes people die from severe cases."

Joshua nodded. "That's true."

"And you have to consider the possibility of suspects other than Marcus," said Beanie, thinking of Fred, the man who'd confronted Pablo at the pool. He thought about introducing Fred as a possible suspect, but he wasn't sure. First of all, he didn't know if Pablo was the punk Fred wanted to teach a lesson. And second, Beanie suspected that Fred wanted the punk beat up, not poisoned. Still—

"But I think I know what my next move is," announced Joshua.

"What's that?" asked Beanie.

"An in-depth background investigation of Pablo," said Joshua. "If I can find out what kind of guy he was, then I might be able to figure out why someone would want to kill him, and if I know why, it might lead me to who murdered him."

12

As Ethan cannonballed into the swimming pool, sending up a wall of water that drenched everyone sitting within a three-foot radius, Beanie sighed and shook his head.

He'd tried to discourage his son from performing dangerous moves in the pool. Ethan had promised he wouldn't break any pool rules. And yet, on a lazy Aerie Islands afternoon, beneath blue skies and bright sunshine, his son broke his promise. Beanie was chagrined, but not surprised. Good thing was, the children surrounding Ethan were delighted by the rainfall of water. The adults sunning and drinking nearby were not exactly amused.

"I think you should apologize to Carmen," suggested Noelle, lying on the chaise next to him in their semi-private cabana.

Beanie grabbed his coconut water from the mini table next to his lounge and took a sip.

His wife's suggestion sounded more like an expectation.

"Even though Joshua and I did nothing wrong," said Beanie, leaning back on the lounge.

"You interrogated her son without her permission," said Noelle.

Beanie glanced toward the lifeguard chair. Marcus Taylor was on duty, scanning the expansive pool area behind mirrored sunglasses.

"It wasn't an interrogation, it was an interview," said Beanie, perturbed by his wife's attitude, and her support of Carmen's position. Noelle had talked to Carmen about the interview the previous evening. After their hour-long conversation, Noelle made it known that she understood Carmen's anger, and felt the same way.

"And Marcus is twenty," continued Beanie. "We didn't need Carmen's permission. Joshua called Marcus and asked to talk with him. Marcus agreed."

"I doubt Marcus agreed to be treated like a criminal in his own home," snipped Noelle.

Beanie glanced at his wife. "Nobody treated him like a criminal."

"Marcus told Carmen that Joshua accused him of killing Pablo."

"What?" Beanie shook his head. "That's not what happened."

"Then what happened?"

Sighing, Beanie said, "Joshua didn't accuse Marcus of murder. But if he had, he would have had good reason to."

"What does that mean?"

Beanie glanced at his wife, not surprised by the frustrated skepticism on her face. "Marcus and Pablo were fighting in the car before it crashed."

"Marcus told you that?"

"No, Daisy Cox, who was also in the car, gave us that information."

"And you're sure she's telling the truth?"

"Elle, you remember how that car was swerving and fishtailing all over the road?" asked Beanie. "You even pointed it out."

Crossing her arms, his wife looked toward the pool. Little Evan was having a blast, giggling and splashing with his playgroup in the kiddie pool, but Beanie could tell his wife's attention was elsewhere. Probably thinking of a way to dispute Daisy's claims. Clearly, because of her friendship with Carmen, Noelle didn't like the idea of Marcus as a potential suspect.

Beanie said, "If it makes you feel better, considering how Pablo died, I do have doubts that Marcus poisoned him, but—"

"But you think it's possible that he did?" asked Noelle.

"Anything's possible," said Beanie. "But is it probable? Did Marcus have motive, means, and opportunity?"

"He's got motive because you think this girl Daisy was telling the truth about Marcus and Pablo fighting?" asked Noelle. "Wasn't there another girl in the car? What did she say about Marcus and Pablo fighting?"

Beanie grabbed the back of his neck, damp from the humid, blustery heat, and massaged it. "Sasha Hidalgo, the other female passenger, claims that Daisy lied. But—"

"But you believe Daisy and not Sasha?"

"It's not that I don't believe Sasha," said Beanie. "Marcus didn't dispute Daisy's story. In fact, he was upset that she hadn't kept her mouth shut."

"You don't know what he wanted her to keep her mouth shut about," pointed out Noelle.

Beanie frowned. "The fact that Marcus wanted her to stay quiet about anything is problematic."

"Problematic?" Noelle scoffed. "You mean suspicious?"

"That word also applies," conceded Beanie. "If Marcus had nothing to do with Pablo's death, then—"

"If he had nothing to do with Pablo's death?"

Beanie threw up his hands. "Elle, I already said that I'm not sure about Marcus poisoning Pablo, but—"

"Oh my God …"

Worried, Beanie glanced at his wife. "What—"

"Look …" said Noelle, inclining her head toward the pool.

Beanie followed his wife's gaze across the sun-dappled water.

At the bottom of the lifeguard chair, two Aerie Islands policemen, along with Detective Gilberto, surrounded Marcus Taylor.

"What's going on?" asked Beanie.

Saying nothing, Noelle shook her head.

As the detective spoke to Marcus, the guests lounging around the pool took notice. A palpable, polarizing silence spread through the atmosphere. Except for the laughter of innocent kids and the splashing of water, there was no sound. The absence of conversation was profound.

Quiet enough to hear the distinctive click when one of the officers placed Marcus in handcuffs.

13

"He's got to stay in jail until his bail hearing," said Carmen Taylor, almost spitting the words as she sat next to Noelle at the large island in the kitchen. "They refused to let him out on his own recognizance."

"That's horrible," said Noelle.

"Not surprising, though," said Carmen, her annoyed expression matching her angry tone.

"When is the bail hearing?" asked Beanie, leaning on the counter next to the oversized Sub-Zero refrigerator. Following Marcus Taylor's ignoble perp walk away from the pool area, the resort guests found their voices. As the din of excited, shocked conversation rose to a fever pitch, Noelle directed Beanie to get the boys while she went to find Carmen.

As it turned out, several other resort employees had informed Carmen about her son's arrest and she had already headed to the police station. Additionally, Noelle learned that Marcus had been charged with the murder of Pablo Lima.

"Two days from now," said Carmen.

"Two days in jail," said Noelle. "Horrible."

Beanie glanced at his wife, wondering if she was thinking back to the time she'd spent behind bars. Unjustly. Beanie's chest tightened when he reflected on one of the worse times of their lives. He'd hated seeing his wife in jail for something she hadn't done. And for what? Because an overzealous detective with a confirmation bias refused to admit he'd been wrong about arresting Noelle for murder.

His wife's pained expression seemed to be on behalf of Carmen's anguish, thank God.

Carmen sighed. "Well, he's been in jail for longer than that before, so I'm not really worried. More concerned about the bail money."

"You think it'll be excessive?" asked Noelle.

Nodding, Carmen said, "Because he's got a record."

"Why was he in jail before?" asked Beanie.

"Because he makes stupid choices and decisions," said Carmen. "Getting caught with drugs. Shoplifting. Fighting."

"Fighting?" echoed Beanie, catching his wife's eye.

Noelle gave him a quick scowl. A warning. But he also saw something else—doubt. Or, rather, a potential willingness to doubt Marcus was some poor, persecuted kid incapable of malfeasance.

Beanie cleared his throat. "Why do the police think Marcus had something to do with Pablo's death?"

Carmen sighed. "Because Marcus's fingerprints were on the bottle of scotch the cops found in the wrecked car. The bottle of scotch contained a poisonous substance which the Medical Examiner said was present in Pablo's bloodstream."

"Pablo drank the poisoned scotch," said Beanie, reflecting on the information. "But I thought all the kids were drinking. Marcus, Sasha, and Daisy, too."

"Yeah, so did I," scoffed Carmen. "But those two witches changed their stories. They went from everybody was drinking to only Pablo was drinking. All of a sudden, they don't like scotch. And Marcus gave Pablo the scotch."

"Which doesn't mean that Marcus poisoned the scotch," said Noelle.

"My son absolutely didn't poison that scotch," said Carmen. "Marcus doesn't drink scotch, either."

"What does Marcus say about all this?" asked Beanie. "Were you able to talk to him?"

"He didn't do it," said Carmen. "But I didn't need my son to tell me that. I know he's not a killer."

"Did the police say anything about a motive?" Beanie asked.

Her mouth pressed into a grim line, Carmen shook her head. "They claim Marcus and Pablo had some sort of beef, which Marcus denies. Did he get along with everybody? Not all of the time. But who does? Coworkers have disagreements."

"Why do the police think Marcus and Pablo had beef?" asked Beanie.

"Because of Daisy and Sasha," said Carmen. "They told the police that Marcus and Pablo were fighting in the car. Now, mind you, that's a different story than what they originally told the cops. Once again, all of a sudden, they remember the guys fighting."

"About what?" Noelle asked.

"They claimed not to know that," said Carmen.

"And Marcus denied fighting Pablo?" Beanie asked.

"He denied the beef," said Carmen. "He came clean about the fight. But he didn't poison Pablo."

"What did they fight about?"

"Marcus told the police that he can't remember. I don't buy it, though," said Carmen. "It probably had to do with Pablo being drunk."

Noelle frowned. "You don't believe Marcus?"

"I know when my son is lying to me," said Carmen. "I just don't know why he's lying."

Beanie rubbed his chin. If Marcus was lying about the reason for his fight with Pablo, was it because that reason might show he had a definite motive to kill Pablo?

"The important thing is clearing my son's name," said Carmen, focusing on Beanie. "That's why I need your help ..."

14

"Carmen Taylor wants us to find evidence to clear Marcus's name," announced Beanie, sitting in the chair adjacent to Joshua's desk in the former intern's roomy cubicle at the *Aerie Observer*.

"Are you serious?" asked Joshua.

Nodding, Beanie chuckled under his breath. Joshua's shock wasn't surprising. Beanie had experienced the same astonishment last night when Carmen requested his help. Although, her request had been more of a demand. She'd said as much.

"You and that kid from the paper like to nose around asking questions," remarked Carmen. "You can put your investigative skills to good use and find out who really killed Pablo."

Floored, Beanie had stammered, desperate to come up with a reason why he shouldn't get involved. He'd glanced at his wife, hoping she would balk at Carmen's request. After all, they were still on vacation.

But Noelle nodded her support of Carmen's idea. "Roland has solved lots of murders."

Blind-sided, Beanie said, "Babe, I don't think—"

"He's the reason why I'm not in jail right now," said Noelle.

"She's giving me way too much credit," protested Beanie. "She's not in jail because she's not a murderer."

"And neither is Marcus," said Carmen.

"Trust me," said Noelle. "If anyone can find out who really killed Pablo, it's Roland."

Knowing he'd been backed into a corner, Beanie gave in and agreed to look into the situation but refused to make any promises about clearing Marcus's name.

Joshua said, "Then let's do it. Let's clear Marcus's name."

Beanie frowned. "But don't you think Marcus is guilty?"

"Whether he's guilty or innocent doesn't matter to my editor," said Joshua, his expression grim. "My last few articles about Pablo's death didn't exactly go viral. My editor wants more engagement. More likes. More comments. More shares. You know how it is."

Nodding, Beanie said, "Yeah, I do. Increasing circulation is a thing of the past. You have to always be breaking the internet."

"I know, right?" Joshua shook his head. "Anyway, so my thought is, I can prove that Marcus is a killer, or I can prove that he's innocent and the cops arrested the wrong man. Either way, I think that story will trend."

"Well, Carmen specifically wants me to clear Marcus's name, so—"

"Which is a totally different but equally compelling angle," said Joshua, tilting his head.

Wary of the shrewd look in the former intern's eyes, Beanie said, "I don't follow ..."

"Maybe my story needs a human-interest element," said Joshua. "A hero to root for. A journalist on vacation gets caught up in a mystery and looks for the truth. Might make a good podcast, too."

"Podcast?" Beanie was confused. "What are you talking about?"

Standing, Joshua said, "I was thinking it might be a good idea to pitch to my editor."

"Whoa, whoa, whoa," cautioned Beanie, wary of the excited gleam in Joshua's slightly manic gaze. "Wait. What are you going to pitch to your editor?"

"I want him to let me report on your efforts to clear Marcus Taylor's name," said Joshua. "I think he'll go for it when I tell him that you've solved lots of murders before—"

"I don't know about that," protested Beanie.

"And you saved my life while solving one of those murders which exposed a Fury follower hiding out in plain sight, and—"

"Joshua, wait a minute." Beanie stood. "I don't think this is a good idea."

"Why not?" Joshua frowned.

"Well, the truth is, I'm not sure I'm the right person to try to clear Marcus's name," admitted Beanie. "I'm not exactly sure that he's innocent."

"Which would be a great story," said Joshua. "You set out to clear Marcus of murder, but find out that he really is the killer."

"But I'm not exactly sure that he's guilty either," said Beanie.

Joshua said, "No matter what, you're looking for the truth. The truth might be that he's guilty. The truth might be that he's innocent. Point is, you could help get justice for Pablo Lima and put a psycho behind bars."

Beanie pinched the bridge of his nose. "Yeah, but … I'm on vacation. A once-in-a-lifetime vacation."

"Yeah, I get that," said Joshua, dropping down into his chair. "You want to enjoy this time with your wife and kids."

Taking his seat, Beanie said, "Nevertheless …"

"Yeah …" prompted Joshua, his eyes alight with hope.

Beanie exhaled. "I did promise Carmen that I would look into things. I didn't promise to clear Marcus's name, but I will do a little investigating."

"And maybe I can tag along while you're looking into things," said Joshua.

Chuckling, Beanie said, "You can help me investigate. And report what we find out."

"That's fair," said Joshua. "So … where do we start?"

"I didn't tell you this because I wasn't sure if it was important, or not," started Beanie. "But, I think I know someone who might have wanted to hurt Pablo …"

15

"Sorry to bother you …" announced Beanie as he and Joshua approached the young man sitting on an overturned wooden crate beneath a large mango tree.

The guy's name was Simba, which Beanie and Joshua had learned from the teenage girl they'd spoken to moments ago. She was the clerk currently on duty at the Aerie Islands Spa Club grocery store, where Beanie had overheard one of the clerks whispering with a man named Fred—the guy who'd confronted Pablo Lima and might have wanted to teach the good-looking lifeguard a lesson.

While driving from the *Aerie Observer* to the resort village, Beanie had given Joshua the details about Fred and the store clerk, including why he wanted to interview the man.

Glancing over his shoulder, Simba scowled. "Can I help you?"

Making his way toward the store clerk, with Joshua following him, Beanie stopped a few feet in front of the young man, who had a cigarette in one hand and a smartphone in the other.

"We spoke a few days ago," said Beanie, thankful for the tree's shade even though it was no match for the humid afternoon temperatures. "You gave me some suggestions about food stalls on the sandbars."

The store clerk took a drag on the cigarette.

Beanie said, "I want to thank you for that. My boys—"

"Man, I got fifteen minutes before I got to go back to work," said Simba, smoke trailing each word. "What do you need?"

"I want to ask you some questions about Fred," said Beanie, mentally preparing himself for the pushback, and how he would circumvent it.

Simba glanced at his phone. "I'm supposed to know who that is?"

"I'm sure you do," said Beanie. "A few days ago, when I came into the store, I saw you talking to him."

Eyes still on the phone, Simba swiped the screen with his thumb. "You sure that was me?"

"How about we not waste the time you still have with this pointless back and forth," suggested Beanie. "If you don't want to answer questions about Fred, then fine. No problem. We'll leave you alone."

Simba took a drag on his cigarette and continued swiping his phone.

"What about Pablo Lima?" asked Joshua. "Can we ask you a few things about him?"

"Management told us not to say nothing to nobody—not even each other—about what happened to Pablo," said Simba, his voice lowered.

As Joshua gave him a worried glance, Beanie said, "I understand. That's why I want to be honest with you. My name is Roland Bean. I'm a reporter with the *Palmchat Gazette*. And this is Joshua Howard, who works for the *Aerie Observer*, and is covering Lima's death."

Shaking his head, Simba looked up at them. "I don't want my name in the paper. Management told us not to talk to the press. I'm supposed to tell you to call the Public Relations office."

Joshua said, "I doubt they'll tell us anything."

The store clerk scoffed. "I doubt they'll answer the phone. But if they do, they're gonna tell you no comment."

"Are you're willing to talk to us?" asked Beanie.

"I'm not a dog," said Simba, scowling as he dropped the cigarette on the ground and then mashed it with the toe of his coral-colored canvas deck shoe. "I don't like nobody trying to put a muzzle on me."

"Then tell me about Fred," said Beanie.

"What do you want to know?"

"Did he have something to do with Pablo's death?"

Simba asked, "What makes you think Fred had something to do with Pablo's death?"

"Fred confronted Pablo about not doing his job," said Beanie. "And then when I overheard him talking to you, he said he wanted to teach some punk a lesson."

"What was that about?" asked Joshua.

"Was Pablo Lima the punk Fred wanted to teach a lesson?" asked Beanie.

Simba exhaled and nodded. "Fred asked me if I knew somebody who could take care of Pablo."

"Did Fred say why he wanted Pablo taken care of?" asked Beanie.

Shaking his head, Simba said, "And I didn't ask. Didn't really care. Figured they had some kind of beef. Pablo is the kind of guy, he had a smart mouth. Had a chip on his shoulder because he had to work for rich people but he didn't like rich people."

"Why did Fred ask you about somebody to take care of Pablo?" Joshua wanted to know. "How do you know Fred?"

"I know all the guests," said Simba, shrugging. "And Fred knows I did a stint in Tiverton."

"Why'd you go to prison?" asked Joshua.

Simba scowled at him. "Why does anybody go to prison? I broke the law. Got caught. Went to prison."

Beanie asked, "Did you know somebody who could take care of Pablo?"

"I gave him a name," admitted Simba.

"And did that person take care of Pablo?" asked Joshua. "Did that person kill—"

"What name did you give Fred?" interrupted Beanie, cutting Joshua a quick look, hoping to convey that the former intern should calm down and be a bit more subtle.

"Dude called Salamander," said Simba before he glanced up at Joshua. "And I don't know if he killed Pablo. You'd have to ask him."

"You know how we can reach Salamander?" asked Beanie.

Simba said, "Salamander works security down at the marina. You should be able to find him there."

16

"Thought you were supposed to be on vacation …" said the raspy voice on the phone.

Beanie chuckled and leaned back in the leather chair behind the large mahogany desk.

After their talk with Simba the store clerk, Joshua was champing at the bit to talk with Salamander, but Beanie cautioned against that knee-jerk reaction. He wanted to vet Simba's information. After all, how did they know the store clerk was telling the truth? Last thing they need was to waste time on a false lead. Joshua was disappointed but agreed that Simba had been surprisingly forthcoming. With little resistance, he'd spilled his guts rather quickly.

Beanie assured Joshua that he could determine if Simba was legit.

He drove the intern back to the *Aerie Observer*, then returned to the Bronson villa at the Aerie Islands Spa Club. Making his way through the wide, opulent hallways, he found the office, a spacious room with the traditional West Indian mahogany, sepia, and bamboo furnishings.

Settled at the desk, Beanie called a man named Lime Shoes, a trusted confidential source who also happened to be a PC-5 gangster. When they'd first met, Lime Shoes doled out information with the intent of making sure Beanie didn't write anything unfair or unflattering about the cartel. Over the years, Beanie and the old gangster had developed a mutual trust and respect.

"I am on vacation," said Beanie. "But it got interrupted by a murder."

"And you have to write about it?"

"Well, the suspect's mother wants me to help clear her son's name," explained Beanie. "And I'm helping a former intern cover the story, so ..."

"Young man, you need to learn how to say no," advised the gangster.

Beanie let out a snorting laugh. "I would have said no if my wife hadn't volunteered my services."

"Well, if your wife told you to do it, then that's another story," said Lime Shoes. "So why are you calling me?"

"You heard of someone called Salamander?" asked Beanie. "Lives in the Aerie Islands and supposedly has ties to the cartel."

"I know who you're talking about," said Lime Shoes.

"So he's connected?"

"Barely," said Lime Shoes, scoffing. "That fool got exiled to Amargo."

"Exiled?" asked Beanie, not recognizing the term. Between Lime Shoes and his wife, Beanie had picked up lots of gang nomenclature, but he couldn't imagine what the old gangster meant.

"Got sent away after he messed up and cost folks a lot of money," said Lime Shoes.

"Interesting," said Beanie.

"He's working off his debt at the marina."

Beanie wanted to ask exactly how Salamander was working off his debt, but doubted Lime Shoes would give up those details. Instead he asked, "You think he'll talk to me?"

"Why you want to talk to him?" demanded the old gangster.

Suddenly wary of Lime Shoe's gruff tone, Beanie cleared his throat. Despite their mutual respect, the old man would not hesitate to remind Beanie that it was dangerous to trifle with him.

"Salamander might have something to do with the murder I'm looking into."

"Is that right?"

Beanie's pulse jumped. "Well ..."

"Because all he's supposed to be doing is working off that debt," said Lime Shoes. "Not supposed to be mixed up in no murder."

"I don't know that he is," said Beanie. "I just need to find out if someone asked him to hurt the guy who was killed, which I doubt he'll tell me, but—"

"This is what you need to do," began Lime Shoes, his voice a low, curt command. "When you talk to him, tell Salamander that I sent you. Then ask your questions and let me know what he says."

Nodding even though Lime Shoes couldn't see him, Beanie said, "Right. Okay. I'll do that."

When Lime Shoes didn't respond, Beanie called his name a few times until he realized the man had hung up.

Exhaling, Beanie ended the call, put his phone on the desk, and leaned back in the chair. He studied the coffered ceiling, following the square pattern of the crown molding as he contemplated what Lime Shoes had told him. Salamander had been exiled to the Aerie Islands. He'd lost the cartel a significant amount of money. Somehow, he'd avoided the dreaded Death List and had been given a chance to make up for his mistakes.

But what would happen to Salamander if he'd had something to do with Pablo Lima's death? Beanie figured the PC-5 had told Salamander to lay low and stay out of trouble. If Salamander had disobeyed orders, would the cartel—

"Are you in the middle of something?" asked Noelle, walking into the office carrying little Evan, who rested his head on her shoulder.

Shaking his head, Beanie stood and walked around in front of the desk. "He's tuckered out, huh?"

Noelle passed Evan to Beanie. "There's just so much to do here and he's having such a good time and he wants to keep up with Ethan, so he's missed a few nap times because he doesn't want to go to sleep and miss out on playtime with his new friends."

"Well, I might need a nap myself," said Beanie, kissing Evan's forehead. "I'll take him out on the terrace and we'll relax for a while before dinner."

Dropping into one of the chairs in front of the desk, Noelle asked, "Were you on the phone?"

Beanie walked back to the large, leather chair, rubbing little Evan's back, trying to soothe the toddler to sleep. "I was talking to Lime Shoes."

Noelle frowned. "Why were you talking to him?"

"I had a question about a guy named Salamander," said Beanie, then went on to give Noelle the details about the PC-5 exile who might have been asked to teach Pablo Lima a lesson on behalf of Fred.

"When are you going to talk to Salamander?" asked Noelle.

Beanie sighed. "Hopefully tomorrow."

"You think you can get him to tell you the truth about Fred?" asked Noelle.

"I'm not sure," admitted Beanie. "I mean, I hope so, but—"

"But, if bringing up Lime Shoes doesn't get Salamander to talk," said Noelle, glancing away. "Then mention Josue Chartres. I'm sure he'll open up and give you the information you need."

Beanie was floored. "You want me to mention your father?"

Noelle gave him a sharp look. "We need to make sure that Marcus isn't railroaded for something he didn't do."

"If Marcus didn't kill Pablo, then the evidence—"

"The police want to close this case as soon as possible," said Noelle. "Carmen told me that the owner of the Aerie Islands Spa Club is good friends with the Prime Minister, who has told the mayor to tell the chief of police that they want Pablo Lima's death solved quickly and quietly."

"Why quickly and quietly?" mused Beanie, planting another distracted kiss on his sleeping son's forehead.

Noelle jumped up and began pacing. "Probably because they know that Fred had something to do with Pablo's death. Or, if not Fred, then some other ultra-wealthy resort guest. Carmen is afraid that the police are trying to protect the real murderer. I hate to think of Marcus going through what I went through. Being accused of a crime you didn't commit."

"Don't remind me," said Beanie, feeling his blood boil when he recalled his wife's false imprisonment.

"Carmen thinks the police and the resort owner are conspiring against Marcus."

Beanie said, "I guess that's possible. It's more likely the cops are suffering from confirmation bias. Pablo was poisoned. The poison was found in the bottle of scotch. Marcus's fingerprints were on the bottle. Marcus and Pablo were fighting. It looks bad."

"The evidence against me looked bad, too," said Noelle, returning to the cane chair. "But I didn't do it. And I don't think Marcus did, either."

"Well, let's see if I can get Salamander to talk to me," said Beanie.

"You have to get him to tell you the truth," said Noelle. "Marcus's freedom may depend on it …"

17

Located on the west side of the island, the Amargo Marina featured floating docks for several types of watercrafts, from sailboats to sleek cabin cruisers, and an expansive harbor capable of berthing two-hundred-foot mega yachts. With the style of a luxurious tropical resort, it boasted various high-end restaurants, a five-star hotel, and a casino—which was where Beanie and Joshua found Salamander.

After breakfast with Noelle and the boys, Beanie stepped out on the terrace to call Joshua. Enjoying the salty, early morning breeze, Beanie brought the former intern up to date, detailing his conversation with Lime Shoes. Twenty minutes later, he and Joshua were cutting through the interior of the island, discussing the case and engaging in speculation about what Salamander might tell them. If he agreed to talk.

Walking along the wide pedestrian pathways, they came across a dock worker who had told them where to find the PC-5 exile. A large, beefy guy with short dreadlocks framing a fleshy, porcine face, Salamander was sitting behind a large circular desk when they arrived. At ten in the morning, the casino was sparsely populated, but the high-pitched dinging of slot machines floated through the air.

"Can I help you gentlemen?" asked Salamander.

Beanie introduced Joshua and himself, then said, "We'd like to ask you a few questions about the murder of a man named Pablo Lima."

Salamander frowned, then looked away. "I'm afraid I can't help you."

"Is the name Pablo Lima familiar to you?" asked Joshua.

"I said I can't help you with that," said Salamander, his expression cold. "Now, if you have questions about the casino, then—"

Beanie said, "Actually, Lime Shoes has a few questions for you."

The exile's eyes widened for a second, or so, before he seemed to gather himself. "Lime Shoes? Am I supposed to know what that is?"

"I think you know him," said Beanie. "But in case you forgot, here's another name you might know—Josue Chartres."

Salamander's Adam's apple bobbed. Clearing his throat, he whispered, "I'll take a break. We can talk outside."

Nodding, Beanie signaled Joshua to follow him out of the casino.

In the fresh air, they walked toward the courtyard, where wooden benches arranged in a square surrounded a natural stone waterfall.

"Why did you bring up Josue Chartres?" asked Joshua.

Beanie took a seat on the bench. "It's complicated ..."

"That's your wife's dad, right?"

Glancing past the boat slips toward the glistening turquoise waters of the Caribbean, Beanie said, "Unfortunately."

Josue Chartres, currently serving a life sentence without the possibility of parole in Tiverton prison, had been a ruthless, diabolical PC-5 assassin. Tasked with executing poor souls on the cartel's gruesome death list, Chartres's reputation still struck fear in the hearts of many island residents.

"Noelle told me to mention her father's name if Salamander refused to talk to us," explained Beanie.

"Mentioning Josue Chartres is going to make Salamander talk?" guessed Joshua.

"Well, we'll find out," said Beanie, as the exile stalked toward them, muscles bulging beneath his security uniform, which seemed a few sizes too small.

Beanie and Joshua made room on the bench so that Salamander

could sit between them. The wood creaked and shifted slightly as the exile settled his muscled girth on the seat.

"What do you want to know about Pablo Lima?" asked Salamander.

Angling toward the exile, Joshua asked, "Did you kill him?"

Beanie tsked beneath his breath.

"What?" growled Salamander. "No, I didn't kill him. Somebody told you I did?"

Beanie said, "Somebody told us they gave your name to a man named Fred who wanted to teach Pablo Lima a lesson."

Salamander scoffed, shook his head. "Man, that dude. Offered me money to beat up Pablo."

"Did you take it?" asked Beanie.

"I'm not a violent person," said Salamander, a hint of offense in his tone. "Despite what I look like. Sure, I go to the gym. Spend a lot of time there. But to stay healthy. I'm not bulking up so I can knock somebody out."

"You weren't a gang enforcer?" asked Joshua.

Salamander scowled at him. "Man, I was an accountant. I moved money. Didn't break no kneecaps."

An accountant, thought Beanie. Made sense. Lime Shoes had told him that Salamander had cost the cartel a significant amount of money. The exile must have overcooked the books somehow.

"I told that dude Fred that I couldn't help him," said Salamander.

"Did Fred tell you why he wanted Pablo beat up?" asked Joshua.

"Claimed Pablo stole something from him," said Salamander, shrugging. "I don't know what. He didn't say. I didn't ask. But I wasn't surprised."

"You weren't surprised about what?" Joshua asked.

"Wasn't surprised Pablo stole from Fred," said Salamander, chuckling under his breath.

"Why not?" Beanie asked.

"Because Pablo was a thief," said Salamander. "That's why he got the job at Aerie Islands Spa Club. So he could steal from all them rich fools."

"How do you know this?" asked Joshua. "Did Pablo tell you?"

Salamander shook his head. "I'm cool with this dude who fenced for Pablo. Fool they call Crooked Lenny."

"Crooked Lenny?" echoed Joshua.

"He sells goat burgers at his food stall on Joker's Cove sandbar," said Salamander.

"Will he be there now?" asked Beanie as he pondered the new information about Pablo Lima. If the good-looking lifeguard had been a thief, dealing in stolen goods, he was bound to have made an enemy or two. Someone else who might have wanted him dead. No honor among thieves, as the cliché went.

"Maybe." Salamander shrugged, then stared at Beanie. "So what questions does Lime Shoes have for me?"

Beanie cleared his throat. "He just wanted to make sure you didn't have anything to do with Pablo Lima's murder."

His expression somewhat relieved, Salamander stood. "Make sure you tell him I had nothing to do with Lima's death. And for that matter, I don't have anything to do with nothing I shouldn't be doing. I'm minding my business."

"I'll be sure to tell him," promised Beanie.

As Salamander walked away, Joshua said, "We need to talk to Crooked Lenny."

Beanie nodded. "I was thinking the same thing."

18

The trip to Joker's Cove sandbar was giving Beanie an eerie sense of déjà vu.

As he and Joshua headed away from the marina, Beanie realized he was driving along the same coastal road he'd been travelling on days ago when he'd seen a car spin out of control before crashing into a cluster of trees.

A car that carried Pablo Lima, Sasha Hidalgo, Daisy Cox, and Marcus Taylor, now sitting behind bars, accused of poisoning Lima. As Beanie came abreast of the exact point of impact, Joshua pointed out the yellow crime scene tape still festooned among the trees. It was a disturbing reminder that immediately brought forth a grim image of Pablo Lima, staggering out of the bushes, bleeding from a head wound.

As he'd travelled with his family that day, Beanie couldn't have fathomed how a car accident would change the trajectory of his vacation. Back then, all he'd seen ahead of him were days of rest and relaxation in luxurious surroundings. Almost a week later, he felt as though he was back at work, investigating a murder case.

"You think we'll have to mention Josue Chartres again?"

Startled from his reverie, Beanie glanced at Joshua. "What?"

"To convince Crooked Lenny to talk," said Joshua. "Will we have to bring up your wife's dad?"

"I hope not," said Beanie.

"You think a fence is gonna talk to us?"

"Stranger things have happened," said Beanie. "Who knows? We just need to find out if anyone else might have wanted Pablo Lima dead."

"But a fence won't want to snitch," said Joshua.

"We can assure him that he'll be an anonymous source," said Beanie. "And we may be able to trick him into telling us what we want to know."

"How?" asked Joshua.

Beanie explained his plan, and Joshua listened attentively.

By the time he finished, Beanie was turning the SUV into the parking lot at the Aerie Ferry Depot. As Beanie parked the SUV, Joshua went to purchase tickets for the next water taxi heading to Joker's Cove. Fifteen minutes later, they were walking across the sandbar, roasting in the unrelenting early afternoon sun.

Shaped like a crescent, Joker's Cove was a small ridge populated by locals, its powdery white sand surrounded by dinghies, rowboats, and jet skis.

"Think that's Crooked Lenny?" asked Joshua, raising a hand to point toward a hand-painted wooden sign in the sand. Roughly fifty feet away, Crooked Lenny's food stall was nothing like the set-ups on Grande Aerie, the largest sandbar, where Beanie had taken his family. Grande Aerie boasted a food midway, where various colorful tents covered stalls featuring a delicious array of mouth-watering delights. Crooked Lenny's Goat & Burgers was basically a bar-b-que pit between two overturned crates.

Trudging across the sand, weaving between clusters of people clad in bikinis and board shorts, Beanie and Joshua made their way to a gnome of a man. About five feet tall, he wore dingy gray board shorts and a white, sweat-stained T-shirt that clung to his drooping paunch. He had a nest of wiry sun-bleached blond hair and pale skin slathered with a thick smear of white sunscreen that coated his face, arms, and chest.

"Sorry to have to tell you this, fellas," began the small man, looking up at them. "Might be about an hour or so wait on the goat burgers.

Meat went rancid overnight. Sent my assistant to the market for more, but—"

"Well, that means you have time to talk," said Beanie.

The man's congenial expression turned dark. "Talk about what?"

"Pablo Lima," said Joshua.

Shaking his head, the small man looked away, then said, "Don't know who that is."

"You're Crooked Lenny, right?" asked Beanie.

The small man scowled. "Some people call me that. I prefer Waylen."

"Waylen?" asked Joshua.

"My given name," said the little man. "Waylen Fleming the Ninth."

"The ninth?" Beanie asked, skeptical.

"It's an old family name," said Crooked Lenny, a hint of pride in his gruff tone. "Now, if you fellas don't want any goat burgers, then there's nothing I can do for you."

"Maybe there's something you can do for yourself," said Beanie, shooting Joshua a quick glance, a signal to the former intern that it was time to enact the plan they'd discussed.

Shading his eyes with his hand, Crooked Lenny asked, "What are you talking about?"

"My name is Joshua Howard," said the former intern. "I'm a reporter at the *Aerie Observer*."

"Reporter?" Crooked Lenny's eyes shifted from Joshua to Beanie and then back to Joshua.

"I'm Roland Bean from the *Palmchat Gazette*."

"What is this about?" demanded Crooked Lenny.

"We have some questions about Pablo Lima," said Joshua.

"Told you I don't know who that is," insisted Crooked Lenny, grabbing a long-handled fork from the side of the bar-b-que pit.

Instinctively, Beanie took a step back, wary of what the little guy might do with the grilling utensil.

"The cops think you might have something to do with Pablo Lima's murder," said Joshua, following the instructions Beanie had given him. If things went as Beanie hoped, they could trick Crooked Lenny into thinking the cops liked him for the murder of Pablo Lima. In an effort to shift blame from himself, the fence might give up the names of other potential murder suspects.

Crooked Lenny stared at them, slack-jawed. "Murder? That's crazy. I didn't kill nobody. Didn't even know Pablo was dead."

"But, you knew Pablo, right?" asked Joshua.

Dragging a hand through his brittle curls, Crooked Lenny said, "Yeah, I knew him. But I did not kill him and if the cops think that, they are wrong."

"So, you and Pablo didn't have beef?" asked Joshua.

"Me and Pablo got along just fine," said Crooked Lenny.

"Well, if you didn't kill him, then who did?" asked Beanie.

"I have no idea," said Crooked Lenny, glaring at them. "What makes you think I would?"

Joshua said, "I think you better come up with someone, other than yourself, who wanted Pablo dead."

"I didn't want Pablo dead," said Crooked Lenny, grounding out the denial through gritted teeth. "And I don't know who did, but …"

"But?" prompted Beanie.

Crooked Lenny frowned. "Pablo had sticky fingers, you know. Liked to take things that didn't belong to him."

"And then he would bring those things to you to fence," said Joshua.

The little man sneered. "Maybe Pablo took something he shouldn't have taken. Something somebody killed him to get back."

"Does that somebody have a name?" asked Beanie.

"Maybe one of them rich fellas at the resort where he worked," said Crooked Lenny. "A lot of the things that Pablo took belonged to those resort guests. Mostly, he took jewelry. Watches. Designer purses. A few times, he took some rare bottles of expensive Scotch."

"Scotch …" Beanie glanced at Joshua. The former intern seemed just as confused and curious as Beanie was. A bottle of Scotch, with Marcus Taylor's fingerprints on it, had been used in Pablo Lima's murder. The libation contained traces of the poison that killed the hunky lifeguard. Beanie couldn't help but wonder about the connection between Pablo Lima stealing scotch and then dying because of it.

"You know who Pablo stole the scotch from?" asked Joshua.

"Never ask who things belong to," said Crooked Lenny. "Always figured Pablo took stuff from one of them rich fellas at the resort, like I said. That's probably who killed him. Wasn't me. I liked Pablo just fine. But rich fellas can be vengeful. You take something from one of them, they gonna make you pay for it. Maybe with your life."

19

Beanie walked down the wide hallway that led to the kitchen.

He'd arrived at the Bronson villa moments ago, fifteen minutes after dropping Joshua off at the *Aerie Observer*, where the former intern had to work on revising several stories for the paper's online version.

Driving back to the resort, Beanie reflected on the speculation session with Joshua. After leaving Joker's Cove sandbar, they rehashed what Crooked Lenny had told them. Most interesting to Beanie was Pablo Lima's theft of expensive scotch, most likely from a rich resort guest. Beanie wondered if the scotch could have belonged to Fred, the wealthy resort guest who'd confronted Pablo. Joshua had thought the same thing. Still, they found it hard to believe that Fred would kill Pablo because of stolen scotch. And yet, Beanie had overheard Fred say he wanted to teach some punk a lesson. Simba the store clerk confirmed Fred had been referring to Pablo.

As he neared the kitchen, Beanie heard voices.

Noelle. Carmen. And a male voice that seemed familiar …

As he stepped into the cavernous kitchen, Beanie's suspicions were confirmed. Sitting at the large island were Noelle, Carmen Taylor, and her son, the main suspect in the murder of Pablo Lima—Marcus Taylor. Immediately, Beanie remembered Marcus from the beach, when he'd huddled with Sasha Hidalgo and Daisy Cox before the three of them hurried away. That image segued into the day he and Joshua had questioned Marcus about the car crash, and what he knew about the death of Pablo Lima. A conversation that had been cut short by Carmen Taylor.

"Beanie, finally you're home," exclaimed Noelle, her expression concerned, as though she'd been waiting for days for his return. "Where have you been?"

Confused by his wife's question, Beanie said, "Joshua and I were following up on the leads I told you about yesterday. The guy named Salamander, remember?"

"Did they have anything we can tell the cops?" demanded Carmen, her gaze as direct as her curt, non-nonsense tone. "Some lead that can clear Marcus's name?"

Glancing at Marcus, whose demeanor could be best described as detached and desolate, Beanie said, "I'm guessing Marcus made bail."

"Cost me an arm, a leg, and an eye," said Carmen, mouth twisted in disgust. "But I wasn't going to let him stay in that jail, where he doesn't belong."

"So what did Salamander say?" asked Noelle.

Beanie stood at the opposite end of the island. "Well, Salamander confirmed that Fred Zachary wanted Pablo beat up because Pablo stole from him, something he learned from a guy called Crooked Lenny."

Noelle and Carmen gave him incredulous looks.

"Crooked Lenny?" asked Noelle. "Are you serious?"

"Actually, his name is Waylen Fleming the 9th," said Beanie.

Carmen scoffed. "That's even worse."

"What did Crooked Lenny tell you?" asked Noelle.

"He confirmed that Pablo stole expensive items from guests at the resort," said Beanie, glancing at Marcus, who seemed to be making an effort not to look at him. "Crooked Lenny fences these items."

"Marcus, I told you not to have anything to do with Pablo," admonished Carmen, glaring at her son.

Beanie asked, "Did you know that Pablo was stealing from the guests?"

Carmen's head whipped toward Beanie. "How would Marcus know about that? My son is not a thief!"

Hands raised, Beanie said, "I didn't say that Marcus—"

"Yeah, I knew …" mumbled Marcus, head lowered.

"You knew Pablo was stealing?" asked Beanie.

"What?" Carmen demanded. "Marcus! Please tell me you were not involved with stealing—"

"I didn't steal nothing," insisted Marcus, raising his head to stare at his mother. "I promise. I never helped Marcus steal, but …"

"But?" prompted Beanie.

Shaking his head, Marcus said, "But I know some guys who did—"

"Who helped Pablo steal from the guests?" demanded Carmen.

His expression pained, Marcus said, "I don't wanna snitch—"

"And I don't want you going to jail for something you didn't do!" Carmen told her son. "Now who are the guys who helped Pablo steal."

Following a defeated exhale, Marcus said, "One of the guys is Kirk South. He's a bartender. The other guy is called PJ. He cleans villas …"

20

At eight in the morning, Kirk South, who worked at the bar in a smaller pool area near the golf course, was cleaning glasses and getting things set up for the mid-morning mimosa crowd.

Beanie and Joshua—who'd showed up at the Bronson villa around seven a.m., in time for breakfast, much to the delight of Ethan and Evan, who monopolized his time with questions and horseplay—strolled to the bar, took seats, and waited for Kirk South to notice them.

As Beanie drove them through the resort in the golf cart, Joshua admitted his worries that Kirk wouldn't talk to them. "Remember, Simba said the resort management told the staff to stay quiet."

"We'll have to see how it goes," said Beanie.

Nodding, Joshua said, "Excuse me …"

Acknowledging them, Kirk South removed a bag of limes from a small refrigerator beneath a sink, and said, "Sorry. We open at eleven."

"We don't want a drink," said Joshua, then introduced himself. "I'm a reporter at the *Aerie Observer.*"

Kirk frowned but said nothing.

"I'm Roland Bean from the *Palmchat Gazette,*" said Beanie. "We were hoping to ask you a few questions about Pablo Lima."

"I don't have anything to say about Pablo Lima," said Kirk, grabbing a knife and a cutting board from a drawer next to the fridge.

"I know the resort management told the employees not to speak to the press," said Joshua.

"That's right, they did," confirmed Kirk. "So I'm not speaking to you."

Scowling, Kirk opened the bag of limes and dumped them into the sink.

Beanie glanced at Joshua. The former intern didn't look as discouraged as Beanie thought he would be, considering that the interview with Kirk South was a bust, over before it even began.

After clearing his throat, Joshua said, "Okay, then, how about you don't speak to us …"

Kirk frowned. "What?"

"How about this," began Joshua, resting his elbows on the bar. "I'll ask you a few yes or no questions. If the answer is yes, you cut the lime in half. If the answer is no, then cut the lime into quarters … okay?"

Beanie thought Joshua's idea was pretty ingenious. But would Kirk South go for it. Technically, he wouldn't be providing a verbal response to Joshua's questions, so he could follow the instructions he'd been given by management to stay quiet.

Kirk glared at Joshua.

Joshua stared back.

Beanie looked at both guys. Kirk was obstinate and reluctant. Joshua seemed determined. Beanie felt as though he was about to witness a duel. The faint strains of calypso music floated from speakers hidden in the trees, lending a strange vibe to the tense moment. Low conversation, a bit of laughter, and the splash of someone jumping into the pool seemed surreal. Frustration made Beanie wish he did have a drink. What was Kirk going to do?

Finally, after what felt like a week, Kirk South cut the lime in half.

Relief flooded Beanie.

"Okay, so … was Pablo Lima stealing from the resort guests?" asked Joshua.

Grabbing another lime, Kirk placed it on the cutting board.

Beanie stared at the shiny green citrus fruit.

Kirk pierced the lime at one end, then sliced it in half.

Holding his breath, Beanie waited.

A few seconds passed, but Kirk didn't make a second cut.

"Did you help him?" asked Joshua.

Scowling, Kirk placed the knife on the cutting board and folded his arms over his chest.

"So, any questions about you being involved, or not, with Pablo stealing from guests is off the table?" asked Beanie.

The bartender said nothing, just glowered at them.

Nodding, Joshua asked, "Did Pablo steal from a guest named Fred? I'm not sure what his last name is …"

Beanie said, "Fred was the guy who confronted Pablo at the pool and security showed up to escort Fred away. You might have heard about that?"

Kirk grabbed a limo and sliced it in half.

"Pablo stole from Fred?"

Kirk pointed to the sliced lime.

"Did he steal scotch from Fred?"

Again, Kirk pointed to the lime.

"So, if you point at the lime, that's yes?" asked Joshua.

"Can't cut up all my limes for you," said Kirk.

Beanie stroked his chin. He was now more inclined to believe that Fred might have had Pablo killed. He'd wanted to teach Pablo a lesson. But after his attempts to get Salamander to beat Pablo up, Fred must have decided to take matters into his own hands.

Joshua asked, voice lowered, "You think Fred could have killed Pablo?"

Kirk pointed to the sliced lime.

21

They found PJ cleaning one of the private massage rooms at the Aerie Petit Spa, nestled in a cluster of lush, verdant palms and tropical bushes, located on the western side of the property.

At the receptionist desk, Beanie made up a story about needing to speak with PJ about cleaning the Bronson villa. The petite, pretty island girl told them PJ was on the second floor finishing the cleaning duties he'd been assigned.

Navigating the warren of hallways, Beanie and Joshua located the housekeeping cart parked against the wall next to an open door. Inside, PJ, a lanky kid with a mohawk of loose curls, mopped the floor and bobbed his head, caught up in whatever music streamed through the small white buds in his ears.

"Excuse us …" said Joshua, raising his voice and waving his hand as he entered the room.

Following the former intern, Beanie stepped over the threshold. The smell of spice, musk, and bleach swirled in the air.

"You have a minute to talk?" asked Joshua, when he'd gotten the kid's attention.

Digging the buds from his ears, PJ dropped them into a large pocket on the front of his coral-colored cotton work shirt. "You the blokes from the newspaper?"

Surprised, Beanie glanced at Joshua.

"How did you know?" asked Joshua.

PJ leaned the mop against the massage table.

"Kirk texted me," said PJ. "Said you were asking questions about Pablo. He figured you would be trying to ask me questions next."

"How did he know that?" asked Beanie.

"Who told you to talk to Kirk? Marcus, right?" PJ chuckled. "Well, if Marcus told you about Kirk, then he probably told you about me."

"Because you and Kirk were working with Pablo to steal from resort guests," said Joshua.

PJ smiled, and shook his head. "Hey, how about this? You answer some questions for me and I'll answer some questions for you. Deal?"

Beanie glanced at Joshua. The former intern looked wary, doubtful. Figuring it might be the only way to get information from PJ, Beanie gave Joshua a slow nod.

Joshua asked, "What do you want to know?"

PJ asked, "Do the cops think I had something to do with Pablo's death?"

Shaking his head, Joshua said, "They think Marcus did it."

"Man, that's stupid." PJ scoffed. "Marcus didn't kill nobody. If anything, Pablo would have killed Marcus."

"Why do you say that?" asked Beanie.

PJ sighed. "Because Marcus found out that Pablo was stealing from the guests and threatened to tell security. So Pablo told Marcus that he would give him a cut if he would stay quiet."

"Hush money," said Beanie, scratching his chin. Marcus hadn't mentioned that interesting detail last night. Beanie wondered why. Had the beef between the lifeguard stemmed from money Pablo owed Marcus? Possibly. Filthy lucre always caused strife and contention.

"Right," said PJ. "Pablo was tired of paying Marcus. He felt like Marcus was blackmailing him. That's why it don't make sense that Marcus killed Pablo. Because you'd think Pablo would kill Marcus so he wouldn't have to pay him no more, right?"

Joshua shrugged. "Unless Marcus killed Pablo because Pablo refused to pay him anymore money."

"Maybe, but I don't think so," said PJ. "Pablo didn't want to pay, but he paid. He was making a lot of money from the stuff he took."

"And so were you," said Beanie.

PJ blinked, then looked away. "I'm not a thief. Sometimes, I forget to lock doors after I clean villas, but that's just an accident. A mistake, you know?"

"You make a lot of mistakes?" asked Joshua.

PJ chuckled. "I am kind of forgetful."

Ignoring his disgust, Beanie asked, "You know anything about Pablo stealing scotch from a resort guest named Fred?"

"I don't know anything about what Pablo stole," said PJ. "Why you ask me that? You think one of the guests killed Pablo? No, I don't think so. These people are so rich, they don't even miss what he took. Don't even know it's gone half the time."

"But you don't think Marcus killed Pablo?" asked Joshua.

"You ask me," said PJ, voice lowered. "It was probably Sasha."

"Sasha Hidalgo?" asked Beanie, confused.

"They were fooling around," said PJ. "But Pablo fooled around with a lot of girls, which Sasha didn't like. They fought a lot. Pablo said she used to threaten him."

"Sasha threatened Pablo?" asked Joshua.

"Sasha is toxic and dramatic," said PJ, shaking his head. "Pablo said she would tell him, if you cheat on me again, I will kill you. Pablo just laughed because girls like Sasha say crazy stuff like that. But, maybe she wasn't just being extra. Pablo is dead. Maybe Sasha made good on those threats …"

22

"PJ is such a disgusting troll," said Sasha Hidalgo. "He actually told you that I threatened to kill Pablo?"

"Did you?" asked Joshua.

Beanie wondered the same thing.

After the conversation with PJ, Beanie and Joshua drove to the Aerie Island Zoo and tracked Sasha down in the herpetology center, where she was having lunch at one of the less crowded zoo restaurants. The sultry blonde—whose roots needed a major touch-up, Beanie noted—wasn't in the mood to talk to them, but when they sat down at her table, she didn't get up and leave.

"No, I didn't," insisted Sasha. "I mean, I didn't mean it, you know? Like, I was just upset with him because he was making a fool of me. Making me look like he owned me. Rumors were going around that I was desperately in love with him and would do whatever he said and that is in no way, shape, or form me, okay? So, I wanted Pablo to set people straight about our relationship. We were just hooking up. I was not in love with him."

"So you threatened to kill him?" Asked Beanie.

Sasha exhaled. "I have a temper, okay? I will admit that, but most of the stuff I say, I don't mean. Ask Daisy how many times I've told her that I would kill her. And she's still alive. She knows I'm all talk, no action. My bark is worse than my bite. Like, I have no bite, okay?"

Beanie glanced at Joshua. The former intern looked as skeptical as Beanie felt.

Sasha cursed under her breath. "Can't believe PJ threw me under the bus! I am going to kill him!"

"You are?" asked Joshua.

"No! I'm not," insisted Sasha, slouching back in the chair. "See what I mean. I blurt out crazy stuff. Whatever is in my head."

For some reason, Beanie was inclined to believe her.

Joshua said, "So you weren't mad at Pablo because he cheated on you?"

Rolling her eyes, Sasha sat forward. "How could he cheat on me? He wasn't my boyfriend, or anything. Yeah, we hooked up once or twice but it didn't mean anything. When I worked there, everybody would hook up with everybody. That's what happens when you work here. It's a gorgeous luxury resort on a beautiful tropical island. Everybody's always drunk and walking around half-naked. It's one of those places where you indulge in your fantasies, you know?"

Beanie scratched his chin. He supposed she had a point. Wasn't he living a fantasy by taking his family to this fabulous place?

"Look, I have to ask you this," began Joshua, his tone wary. "And I know it'll probably upset you, but—"

"No, I didn't kill Pablo," said Sasha, giving Joshua a withering scowl. "That's what you were going to ask me, right? Who told you I did? PJ? He's such a toad."

"Do you think Marcus killed Pablo?" asked Beanie.

Sighing, Sasha shook her head. "I don't think so."

"You have any idea who it was?" asked Joshua.

"Yeah, but I'm sure no one would believe me," said Sasha, flipping a column of blonde hair over her shoulder. "He's one of the guests here. His name is Fred Zachary."

"Fred Zachary," repeated Beanie, glancing at Joshua, who was making a note of the name in his phone. Making a mental note to remember the last name, Beanie was fairly confident Sasha was referring to the same Fred who'd confronted Pablo, then asked Simba the store clerk to help him find someone to teach Pablo a lesson.

"Why do you think Fred Zachary killed Pablo?" asked Joshua.

"Because Pablo was hooking up with Fred's wife," said Sasha, a sly, mischievous glint in her dark eyes. "Fred caught them in bed together …"

23

"I don't think Mr. Zachary killed Pablo," said Daisy Cox, hugging her arms around her frail frame as she paced back and forth across the living room of her small apartment.

Following their conversation with Sasha Hidalgo, Joshua suggested they speak with Daisy Cox, to see if she might have more information about Pablo and Fred Zachary's wife. As they drove to Daisy's place, Joshua speculated that Fred wanted to teach Pablo a lesson because the lifeguard had fooled around with his wife. Beanie agreed. A cheating spouse might incite a man to murder. His wife's infidelity was a stronger motive for Fred's desire to see Pablo dead. It made more sense than killing a man over a bottle of stolen scotch.

"Was Sasha wrong about Pablo having an affair with Fred Zachary's wife?" asked Joshua.

Daisy shook her head. "Pablo did hook up with Mrs. Zachary. But so did a lot of guys. And Mr. Zachary wasn't faithful to her, either. They have a sort of weird marriage."

"What kind of weird marriage?" asked Joshua.

Beanie was sure he knew what Daisy Cox meant, but he waited for the slight girl to confirm.

Her expression pained, as though it irritated her to explain herself,

Daisy shrugged. "You know … one of those marriages where they let each other cheat."

"An open marriage," said Joshua.

Daisy sighed. "Right."

"Interesting," remarked Beanie.

Sinking down onto the lumpy divan across from the couch where Beanie sat next to Joshua, Daisy said, "It doesn't make sense that Mr. Zachary would want to kill Pablo for hooking up with his wife when he was hooking up with other women."

"Maybe it doesn't," said Joshua.

Beanie sighed under his breath. If Fred Zachary and his wife had an open marriage, then Beanie supposed infidelity could no longer be considered Fred's motive. Still, he had trouble thinking a man would kill because of stolen liquor.

Joshua asked, "What about Sasha Hidalgo?"

Daisy frowned. "What do you mean?"

"You think she could have killed Pablo?" asked Joshua. "They hooked up a few times. Sasha apparently threatened to kill him."

Waving a dismissive hand, Daisy said, "Sasha's always threatening people. She's all talk. I doubt she did it."

"You have any idea who killed Pablo?" Beanie asked.

Daisy exhaled. "Not really. And I have problems believing he was killed. I know the cops say somebody poisoned him, but what if it was an allergic reaction, or something. Maybe it was alcohol poisoning. Like from drinking too much scotch. Pablo always drank too much. He was a mean drunk. Alcohol made him violent."

"Is that why Pablo and Marcus were fighting?" asked Joshua.

Jumping up, Daisy started to pace again. "They were fighting about money."

"Money?" asked Beanie, glancing at Joshua. The former intern raised an eyebrow.

"Marcus was telling Pablo that he wanted his money," said Daisy, rubbing her pale, freckled arms. "I guess Pablo had borrowed money from Marcus. But Pablo said he wasn't giving Marcus anything. And then, they started speaking patois."

"Patois?" questioned Joshua.

Beanie knew what Daisy meant, as he was fluent in the island pidgin himself, which was a mix of Creole, Portuguese, and broken English.

"I wasn't born on the island, so I don't understand it," said Daisy. "Neither does Sasha. She's from Puerto Rico. Anyway, I don't know what they were saying to each other but I could tell they were arguing. And then the arguing just exploded into a physical altercation. And ... I already told you the rest."

Joshua asked, "You think Marcus could have killed Pablo."

Daisy shuddered. "I hope not. I don't want to think he did, but ..."

"But?" prompted Beanie.

"But I keep thinking about when me and Sasha climbed down to the beach," said Daisy, her lower lip quivering. "Marcus stayed up there with Pablo. And I don't know what happened between them during that time. I don't want to think that Marcus ... hurt Pablo ... but Marcus was so mad at him. Maybe mad enough to kill him ..."

24

"You think Daisy Cox was right?" demanded Noelle. "You think Marcus was so mad about some money Pablo owed him that he killed Pablo?"

Beanie sighed and glanced at his wife.

Lying in the plush king-sized bed, after a long day of sleuthing and then spending quality time with his boys at the beach, Beanie wanted to rest his weary mind and body. He needed to sleep. But Noelle wanted to discuss the murder case against Marcus.

"Well, Pablo was stealing from the resort guests," said Beanie. "Several sources have corroborated that, including Marcus himself. And it looks like Marcus was accepting hush money from Pablo. But then Pablo got tired of paying Marcus."

"Which gives Pablo more of a motive to kill Marcus," said Noelle.

Recalling that PJ, the janitor, had said the same thing, Beanie said, "Right. But—"

"And I think that guy Fred has a motive," interrupted Noelle. "Sure, maybe they had an open marriage, but men don't like when women cheat on them. And who knows, maybe Fred's wife had fallen in love with Pablo."

Considering the possibility, Beanie said, "Maybe, but—"

"Now it makes sense why Fred confronted Pablo at the pool," said

Noelle. "He was probably mad because Pablo and his wife had fallen in love. I've read about these open arrangements."

Shocked, Beanie stared at his wife. "You have?"

Nodding, she said, "Most of the time, the couple agrees to keep the outside relationships casual. But, problems arise when one of the spouses falls for someone else. I'll bet that's what happened."

Beanie said, "Or, maybe Fred was upset about Pablo stealing his scotch."

Noelle scoffed. "You don't really think that, do you?"

"Actually, I do find it odd," said Beanie.

"And remember, Pablo had been drinking scotch when he died," said Noelle.

"The poison was in the scotch," said Beanie.

"And the bottle of scotch probably belonged to Fred," said Noelle.

"But Marcus's fingerprints were on the bottle," said Beanie.

"Which doesn't mean he poisoned the scotch," said Noelle. "Just means he picked up the bottle."

Beanie sat up. "You know … I should have asked Marcus if he drank some of the scotch. I don't think I ever did."

"If Marcus drank some of the scotch, wouldn't he have been poisoned, too?"

"Not if he poisoned the scotch after he drank from it," said Beanie.

Noelle bit her bottom lip. "I guess that's possible, but—"

Beanie's phone beeped, cutting off his wife.

"Text message?" asked Noelle.

Nodding, Beanie reached over and grabbed his phone from the bedtable.

His heart jerked as he read the message.

JOSHUA HOWARD

Can you give me a call. Bad news.

"What's the matter?"

Beanie cleared his throat. "It's from Joshua. Says bad news."

"Bad news about what?"

"Not sure."

"Call him and see," Noelle said.

Minutes later, Beanie had the former intern on the line.

"Friday told me that the cops have surveillance video of Marcus stealing a bottle of scotch from Fred Zachary's villa," said Joshua.

"You're kidding," said Beanie.

Joshua said, "Wait, it gets worse."

"How much worse?" asked Beanie.

"What's worse?" asked Noelle, placing a hand on his shoulder. "What's going on?"

"The video shows Marcus stealing a bottle of scotch from one of the villas. He then removes a small packet from the pocket of his shorts," said Joshua. "He opens the packet, and then dumps the contents into the bottle of scotch …"

25

"I didn't kill Pablo," insisted Marcus Taylor, head lowered.

Beanie stared at the young lifeguard whose bleary eyes and haunted expression worried him.

Harsh, early morning sunlight drifted through the wall of French doors in the breakfast nook, where Beanie, Noelle, Marcus, and his mother Carmen sat at the round orange wood table.

Following the shell-shocking conversation with Joshua the night before, he and Noelle had spent several hours lamenting Marcus's fate while at the same time trying not to think the worse. After a fitful night's sleep, Beanie woke early to find his wife was already up, making coffee in the kitchen. She'd been in contact with Carmen. The activities coordinator and her lifeguard son were headed to the Bronson villa to strategize. Groggy and confused, Beanie poured coffee into a mug and wondered what kind of strategy they were supposed to come up with.

The evidence against Marcus, which had been bad but circumstantial, was now worse and concrete. The only strategy Beanie could think of was a plea deal.

Beanie said, "Marcus, the video shows that you stole a bottle of scotch, put poison in it and—"

"Wasn't poison," said Marcus, elbows propped on the table, hands cupped over his head, shielding his face from scrutiny.

"Then what was it," demanded Carmen, her voice hoarse and shrill, as she glared at her son. "What was in that packet that you poured in that bottle if it wasn't poison?"

Beanie wondered the same thing. A quick glance at his wife told him she held the same curiosity.

"It was cannabis powder," mumbled Marcus.

"Cannabis powder?" echoed Noelle.

"Drugs?" Carmen's voice rose in incredulity and irritation. "Seriously, Marcus! Drugs! Why would you do that? What were you thinking? Or, were you thinking? Obviously not!"

"I don't understand," said Beanie. "Why would you put cannabis power in the scotch?"

"We always do that," said Marcus. "We add it to liquor. It acts like a mood enhancement."

"You mix drugs with alcohol?" Carmen scowled at her son. "Are you crazy?"

"That could be potentially dangerous," said Noelle.

Beanie noted his wife's cautious tone. As a pharmacist, she was well aware of the effects of psychoactive drugs and alcohol, but she obviously didn't want to suggest what they were probably all thinking— that Marcus's cannabis and scotch cocktail produced some sort of adverse effect on Pablo, causing his death.

"Never was dangerous before," said Marcus, shaking his head. "We always add cannabis powder and it never killed nobody."

"Well, this time it did, Marcus!" shouted Carmen, banging the table before she burst into sobs.

Noelle jumped up and went to her friend. Wrapping a supportive arm around the crying, desolate woman, she helped Carmen to her feet and led her out of the nook.

Beanie took a deep breath. "Marcus—"

"I didn't kill Pablo," Marcus said, grounding the words through gritted teeth as he glared at Beanie. "I don't know how he got poisoned but it wasn't the cannabis powder."

"Okay, okay," said Beanie holding up his hands, trying to deescalate the tension. "If you say you didn't poison him, then—"

"Had to be that old rich dude who we stole the scotch from," said Marcus.

"Fred Zachary," said Beanie. "He gave the police the interior surveillance video of you taking the scotch."

"Yeah, I know," said Marcus. "And yeah, I took the scotch. There's no way I can say I didn't. My lawyer says it's clearly me on the tape."

"Why do you think Fred Zachary poisoned Pablo?" asked Beanie, wanting to hear the young lifeguard's theory, even though he believed it might be possible.

"Cause Pablo had something on him," said Marcus.

"You mean the open marriage stuff?" asked Beanie.

Marcus frowned. "Open marriage? They got an open marriage?"

Confused, Beanie asked, "Don't they? I mean, did you know?"

Shaking his head, Marcus said, "Don't know nothing about they marriage."

"Was Pablo involved with Mrs. Zachary?" asked Beanie.

Nostrils flaring as though he smelled something putrid, Marcus said, "That old lady? She could be Pablo's mom."

"True, but …"

"Pablo didn't hook up with old ladies," said Marcus. "Some of them wanted to get with him. Me, too. All them old rich ladies want to hook up with some young guy, but … Pablo wasn't interested in that. Pablo was only interested in money.

"Which was why he would steal things from the villas," said Beanie.

Marcus nodded.

Beanie said, "And he paid you to stay quiet about his illegal activities, right?"

Exhaling, Marcus looked away.

"That's why you and Pablo were fighting in the car, wasn't it?" asked Beanie. "Pablo owed you money for staying quiet but he was tired of paying you. Did you threaten to go to the police?"

"Why would I go to the police?" Marcus scoffed. "And tell them what? This guy won't pay me to stay quiet about how he steals stuff from villas? They would have locked me up, too."

Nodding, Beanie said, "Charged you with conspiracy, probably."

"Look, I know it was wrong to stay quiet about what Pablo was doing," said Marcus. "I know it was wrong to take his money and keep my mouth shut."

"Why did you?" asked Beanie.

Leaning back, Marcus shook his head. "Don't know. Guess I just wanted the money."

Beanie sighed. "Tell me something. What really happened the day Pablo died? You and Daisy and Sasha have told different stories and changed your stories and—"

"Okay, here's the truth," began Marcus. He blew out a breath, then said, "Me, Pablo, Daisy, and Sasha went to the Zachary villa that day. Pablo wanted some scotch—not to sell, for us to drink—and Mr. Zachary has the best scotch. Pablo found out that Mr. Zachary would fly to Scotland and buy it from there. Anyway, Pablo told me to get the scotch from the liquor cabinet in Mr. Zachary's office, which I did."

"And that's how you were seen on the surveillance camera stealing," said Beanie.

"Right," said Marcus. "While I was still in the office, I put the CBD powder in the scotch. Then I took it out to the pool, were Pablo, Daisy, and Sasha were swimming. We all took some swigs of scotch, then I took the bottle back into the house. Then I went back to the pool to chill with the rest of them. Then we decided to leave because we didn't know when the Zacharys would be coming back. So Pablo told me to grab the scotch, which I did."

"And then the four of you got into Sasha's car …"

Marcus nodded. "And then me and Marcus started arguing. He swung at me, so I swung back and that's when he lost control of the car. Then we all got out of the car. Sasha was screaming and cursing at Pablo for wrecking her car. Then Pablo got in Sasha's face, so I pushed him back. He swung at me again. I swung back. We pushed each other, then Pablo clutched his stomach, bent over and then took off into the bushes.

I figured he was gonna get sick, so I just climbed down to the beach where Sasha and Daisy were …"

"And you left him there?"

Sighing, Marcus said, "I figured he'd be okay. Didn't think he had been poisoned. Just thought the scotch made him sick because he drank too much."

"How do you know how much he drank?"

"When I grabbed the scotch for Pablo when we left," said Marcus, "he yanked it from me and started drinking. He kept drinking."

"What about you, Sasha, and Daisy?" asked Beanie, rubbing his jaw.

"I don't know if they drank any more of the scotch," said Marcus. "Can't remember. I didn't drink any more of it."

Carmen stomped back into the room, Noelle following close behind.

"The lawyer called. He needs to talk to you," said Carmen, glaring at Marcus. "Let's go."

Sighing, Marcus rose to his feet. "Mom, I—"

"Don't, okay," warned Carmen, pointing an accusing finger at him. "Let's just go."

Pivoting, Carmen stomped out of the breakfast nook while Marcus shuffled behind her, hands shoved into the pockets of his windbreaker, head hung low.

Noelle walked over to Beanie. "What a nightmare. I can't imagine what she's going through."

"Let's hope we never have to," said Beanie, slipping an arm around his wife.

Resting her head against his shoulder, Noelle said, "Let's go enjoy our little boys while they're still innocent little boys."

26

"Feels like forever since we saw you!" exclaimed Flo Taylor as she took a sip of her drink.

"I guess a week maybe," said Beanie, trying to remember when he'd encountered the wealthy ex-pats in the resort grocery store. The same day he'd overheard Fred Zachary requesting help to teach Pablo Lima a lesson.

"I'm shocked we're still here," said Flo, lounging on the chaise, oversized sunglasses covering half her face.

Beanie had been surprised to get a call from Chuck.

After Carmen and Marcus left—both of them still raw with pain and not speaking to each other— he and Noelle enjoyed breakfast on the patio with the boys. When they were full of waffles, goat sausage, and fruit, Noelle took them to the play center.

Beanie was about to call Joshua when the phone rang.

Chuck's booming, jovial voice jolted him, as did the man's request that Beanie join him and Flo at their villa. Beanie wasn't exactly in the mood, but Chuck told him they wanted to talk about the situation with Fred Zachary. Recalling that in the past, the couple had provided valuable information about rich people that Beanie wouldn't have access to, Beanie decided to find out what they had to say. It would mean enduring their elitist obtuseness but it would be worth it if they knew something that might help Marcus's case.

"Sure you don't want a Palmito, Beanie?" asked Chuck, standing at the outdoor bar, mixing a bit of pineapple juice into his white rum.

"I'm okay," said Beanie. Despite being on vacation, eleven in the morning was still too early, for him at least, for alcohol. Chuck and Flo didn't feel the same. Judging from Flo's languid posture and slightly slurred voice, Beanie would wager they'd started the morning with a Bloody Mary or Irish coffee.

Flo took a drink, then said, "So, the reason I told Chuck that we had to talk to you is because we think poor Matthew has been falsely accused."

Confused, Beanie asked, "Matthew?"

Flo said, "The young man arrested for murder. The police think he killed his coworker, the other young lifeguard. You must know who I'm talking about."

"Oh, you mean Marcus," said Beanie.

Lowering her sunglasses to the tip of her nose, Flo regarded Beanie with skeptical eyes. "I thought it was Matthew. I'm sure that's what I read in the paper this morning."

"No, it's Marcus," said Beanie, telling himself not to chuckle at Flo's penchant for getting names wrong. "Marcus Taylor."

"Well, if you say so," said Flo, pushing her glasses back up.

Drink in hand, Chuck walked to the chaise where Flo lounged and sat on the end.

"As Flo was saying," said Chuck. "We think the police arrested the wrong person."

Nodding, Flo took another drink, and said, "They should be looking at Fred Zachary."

"Why do you say that?" asked Beanie, deciding to keep his suspicions to himself.

"Rumor has it," said Chuck, leaning forward toward Beanie, his voice lowered, "that Fred Zachary has poisoned before."

"Supposedly, that's how he got rid of his first two wives," said Flo. "Both of whom were very wealthy."

"Who told you this?" asked Beanie, cautioning himself not to get too excited. The information would have to be verified. Still, if true, it was explosive.

"People talk," said Chuck. "The Zachary villa belonged to the first wife. Fred's money comes from the women he married and then summarily got rid of. Allegedly."

"Supposedly, he poisoned the first two women with antifreeze," said Flo, finishing her drink. "It's known to have a sweet taste and easy to mask in a sweet drink …"

Disturbed, Beanie nodded. "Yeah, I've heard that."

Chuck said, "Maybe you should tell the police."

"We'd hate to see the wrong person go to jail for something they didn't do," said Flo.

Beanie asked, "Did you tell the police about Fred Zachary?"

"No, we haven't had time," said Flo. "We've been so busy."

"And we'll be leaving in a few days," said Chuck, chugging the remainder of his Palmito. "And I doubt we'll have time to call the police before we go."

"Fix me another, dear," said Flo, smiling as she held out her empty glass to her husband.

"Of course, love," said Chuck, standing. He took the glass and strolled back to the bar, humming a jaunty salsa tune.

"Make sure you tell the police to check the victim for antifreeze," advised Flo.

27

"I think your friends were right," said Joshua, spinning in the swivel chair to face Beanie.

Beanie sat in the guest chair in Joshua Howard's spacious cubicle, which Beanie still couldn't believe and hated feeling jealous about, but how could he not, considering the tiny cube and small desk he would return to when his vacation was over?

"I did the research you told me," said Joshua.

Once he'd left the Taylor villa, Beanie jumped in the golf cart, motored back to the Bronson villa, and sent Joshua an email. After detailing his conversation with the wealthy ex-pats, he'd asked Joshua to determine if he could corroborate their story. If Fred Zachary had, allegedly, killed two of his wives, maybe there was some news article chronicling the suspicions.

"First, I searched several marriage databases to find out the names of Fred Zachary's wives," began Joshua, eyes alight with pride and excitement. "Once I found the former spouses—both deceased—I looked up their death certificates."

"Was a cause of death listed?" asked Beanie.

Nodding, Joshua turned back to his computer and opened a file. "Ethylene glycol poisoning for the first wife."

"Antifreeze," said Beanie.

Clicking his mouse, Joshua opened more files. "I also was able to get the 911 call that Fred made. He told the dispatcher that he'd come home, found his wife unresponsive, with a bottle of antifreeze and a suicide note next to her body."

Beanie was floored. "You're kidding …"

Shaking his head, Joshua said, "Nope. But things get more interesting. I found several articles about the first wife's death. Apparently, the first wife's son told the police that the suicide note was forged. The cops looked into it, but nothing came of it. The son hired a handwriting analysis, who declared, via affidavit, that the note was fake."

"Did the police reopen the case?"

"They did, but then Fred Zachary hired his own handwriting analyst, who said the note was real."

"So it would come down to whose expert do you believe," said Beanie.

"Cops didn't think there was enough evidence to bring charges against Fred," said Joshua. "It didn't help that the first wife suffered from extreme depression. She was seeing several therapists. And she'd attempted suicide in the past before she married Fred."

Beanie scratched his chin. "So, maybe Fred didn't poison her."

Joshua faced Beanie again. "Or maybe Fred took advantage of her mental illness, murdered her, and then made it look like she'd killed herself."

"Maybe," said Beanie. "What about the second wife?"

"Apparently, she died from injuries sustained from a fall down the stairs after she'd had too much to drink," said Joshua.

"Sounds fishy," said Beanie. "What did the cops think?"

"Well, the cops didn't get involved," said Joshua. "Not initially anyway."

"What do you mean?"

"The second wife's family did alert the authorities to tell them they found her death suspicious," said Joshua. "But, by the time they found out that she was dead, it was months later and Fred had already had her cremated."

Scoffing, Beanie said, "Which means exhuming the body to test for any suspicious substances was out of the question."

Nodding, Joshua said, "The family accused him of paying a crooked doctor to fake the death certificate so Fred could claim the body and have it cremated."

"Very shady," noted Beanie.

Joshua said, "But it makes me wonder if Fred Zachary could have poisoned Pablo. I mean, think about it. You told me that Marcus added cannabis powder to the scotch. I researched the powders. A lot of them are flavored."

"And antifreeze supposedly has a sweet taste," said Beanie.

"Exactly," said Joshua. "Which means Pablo might not have suspected there was something wrong with the liquor. He might have attributed any sweet flavor to the cannabis powder."

"But when would Fred have spiked the scotch with antifreeze?" mused Beanie. "Sometime before Marcus stole it?"

"That's what I'm thinking," said Joshua. "Based on what Crooked Lenny told us, it's possible that Fred suspected Pablo was stealing his scotch. Maybe he decided to teach Pablo a lesson by poisoning him. And who knows? Maybe Fred didn't plan to poison Pablo to death. Remember, he wanted Salamander to beat up Pablo."

"So the antifreeze in the scotch was a Plan B," said Beanie, rubbing his jaw.

"You know, whether or not Fred and his wife were cheating on each other is anybody's guess," said Joshua. "Sasha said Pablo was hooking up with Fred's wife. Marcus said Pablo wasn't interested in older women, so maybe Fred wasn't mad at Pablo for fooling around with his wife."

"But maybe he didn't want Pablo stealing the scotch," said Beanie. "So if some of the scotch made Pablo sick, maybe he would think twice about stealing it."

"However, Fred probably didn't know that Marcus would add the cannabis powder," Joshua said. "That plus scotch plus antifreeze equaled a lethal combination."

"You know what we need to do?"

"We need to talk to Fred," answered Joshua. "Question is, will he talk to us?"

Standing, Beanie said, "There's only one way to find out …"

28

"Good afternoon, can I help you?" asked a petite, demur woman dressed in a coral-colored short-sleeved cotton dress.

The villa housekeeper, figured Beanie before he introduced himself, and Joshua.

"Is Mr. Zachary available?" asked Joshua.

Her dark, almond-shaped eyes slightly suspicious, she asked, "And why do you need to see Mr. Zachary?"

"Well, as Mr. Bean said, I'm a reporter at the *Aerie Observer*," began Joshua. "I'd like to ask Mr. Zachary—"

"Who's at the door, Mabel?" bellowed the terse demand from the recesses of the expansive foyer, somewhere behind the maid.

Her expression stricken, the maid opened her mouth but was suddenly pulled back as the door opened wide. A short, stocky guy with thin hair and saggy, leathery skin scowled at them. Beanie recognized him as the man who'd confronted Pablo at the pool—Fred Zachary.

"Get back to work," Zachary barked at the maid, who nodded and scurried out of sight. Stepping over the threshold, Zachary forced Beanie and Joshua to take several steps back as he closed the door behind him, letting them know he wasn't going to invite them in for a friendly chat.

"Can I help you?" demanded Zachary, his gruff tone indicating his annoyance.

"I'm Joshua Howard," said the former intern. "I work as an investigative reporter for the *Aerie Observer.*"

"And?" Zachary folded his arms across his chest.

"I just have a few questions about the video surveillance you provided to the police in connection with the Pablo Lima murder," said Joshua.

"What kind of questions?" asked Zachary.

"Why did you give the police the video?" asked Joshua.

"Right thing to do," said Zachary. "Trying to make sure a murderer doesn't go free. Doesn't get to work at this resort, roaming around, looking for victims."

"How long did you have the video before you gave it to the police?" asked Beanie.

Zachary exhaled. "Day I turned it over to the cops was the day I found it."

"Really?" asked Joshua.

"It was sort of an accident," said Zachary. "I was actually looking for proof that Pablo Lima had stolen several bottles of rare, aged malt scotch from my liquor cabinet."

"Why were you looking for that?" asked Beanie.

"I suspected Pablo Lima was stealing from me," said Zachary. "I had the video surveillance installed and hoped to catch him in the act so I could report him to the police. When he passed away, I decided to file an insurance claim instead, to recover my losses—which were substantial—on the scotch that punk stole from me."

"So your insurance company is requiring proof that the scotch was stolen," said Beanie, noting Zachary's use of the word punk, which brought to mind what he'd overheard the little corpulent man telling Simba, the store clerk. *That punk needs to learn that he can't disrespect me. He needs to be taught a lesson.*

Zachary nodded. "But every time I reviewed the footage, which was every day after I had the cameras installed because I had no idea when Lima was sneaking into my villa, there was no evidence of his thievery."

"Maybe because Pablo wasn't stealing your scotch," said Joshua.

Zachary expelled a short scoffing snort. "Or maybe because my wife knew Pablo was stealing and erased the video evidence so that punk wouldn't go to jail."

"Why would she do that?" Beanie asked.

"She and Lima were fooling around," said Zachary. "I'm sure that's how he was sneaking into my villa. She denies it, of course."

"But she didn't erase the video of Marcus stealing your scotch," said Joshua.

Zachary shrugged. "She wasn't fooling around with him."

"Is that why you wanted to teach Pablo Lima a lesson?" asked Beanie, deciding to go for the direct approach, since Zachary had introduced the subject of his wife's infidelity.

Eyes narrowed, Zachary said, "Not sure what you're talking about."

Beanie said, "I spoke with someone who told me that you wanted Pablo Lima beat up."

"Who is someone?" asked Zachary, sneering.

"Can't reveal my sources," said Beanie.

"You can't trust your sources, either," said Zachary. "Someone told you a lie."

"But you were upset with Pablo Lima for stealing your scotch and fooling around with your wife," said Joshua,

"So what if I was?" challenged Zachary.

"So that gives you a motive for murder," Joshua said.

"You don't know what you're talking about," Zachary said. "Sure, I wanted Lima fired. I wanted him in jail. But I didn't want him dead."

"You know Pablo Lima was poisoned, right?" asked Joshua.

Fred Zachary frowned as splotches broke out across his cheeks.

"The police haven't determined what the toxic substance was," said Joshua. "But I was thinking it might have been antifreeze."

The pink splotches on Zachary's skin darkened. "Antifreeze."

"Ethylene glycol," said Beanie.

"Isn't that what killed your first wife?" asked Joshua.

His jaw clenched, face now as red as a boiled lobster, Fred Zachary turned, stepped back into his villa, and slammed the door.

29

As little Evan ran around the kitchen squealing, his bare feet slapping the hardwood floor, and Ethan sat on a stool at the massive center island, swiveling in circles, Beanie grabbed a plastic tub of chocolate ice cream from one of the Sub-Zero freezers.

Ice cream, whipped cream, chocolate sauce, and sprinkles were a fitting treat, considering all the investigating he and Joshua had done earlier. Following their confrontation with Fred Zachary, Beanie called it a day, even though it was only one in the afternoon. Joshua seemed a bit worse for the wear, and eager to catch up on his other assignments. They agreed to reconvene tomorrow.

Deciding to give himself a break from sleuthing and switch back into vacation mode, Beanie returned to the Bronson villa. Noelle and the boys were lounging around, watching a movie. Beanie joined them for the second half of a Pixar flick his kids had seen a dozen times and knew by heart.

After the movie, Beanie volunteered to take the boys for a swim in the villa's pool while Noelle went to a yoga class on the beach. Two hours horsing around with his kids proved to be soothing and peaceful, a perfect balm to remind him to enjoy himself. Eventually, the boys grew tired of the water. They had lunch, then napped, and woke up craving something sweet.

"Daddy …" said Ethan.

"Yeah, buddy," said Beanie, crossing to the pantry doors, which he opened. He entered a room about half the size of the kitchen, stocked with enough food to replenish the shelves of a small store.

"Can we go to Tiverton?"

Beanie almost dropped the jar of sprinkles he'd swiped from one of the shelves.

Pivoting, he hurried out of the panty. "What did you say?"

Swiveling to the right and then to the left, Ethan said, "Can we go to Tiverton?"

"Tiverton!" sang Evan, wrapping his arms around Beanie's left leg. "Tiverton!"

Reaching down to pick up Evan, Beanie stared at Ethan. "Why would you want to go there?"

"I want to get down, Daddy," pouted little Evan, squirming in Beanie's arms. "Put me down!"

Ethan stopped swiveling, jumped to his knees on the stool, and rested his elbows on the island. "We need to go to Tiverton to visit Marcus when he goes to jail, Daddy!"

"Marcus goes to jail!" sang Evan, giggling. "Marcus goes to jail!"

"What makes you think Marcus is going to jail?" asked Beanie, walking to a section of overhead cabinets. "Wait a minute. How do you know Marcus?"

"Miss Carmen is his mom!" said Ethan. "She was crying a lot. Mommy hugged her and said, don't cry, it's going to be okay. But Miss Carmen said Marcus is going to go to prison because he is stupid! Is that true, Daddy? Is Marcus going to Tiverton because he is stupid?"

"Tiverton stupid!" echoed Evan. "Tiverton stupid!"

Beanie took a deep breath, trying to calm his slamming heart. His son's mention of the notorious maximum-security prison brought to mind Josue Chartres. Beanie's father-in-law. His boys' grandfather. The ruthless assassin. For some inexplicable reason, Beanie had thought Ethan wanted to go to Tiverton to visit Josue. Which was ridiculous. The boys didn't know anything about the heartless killer. Noelle was adamant that the kids would never have any contact with their infamous grandfather.

"Daddy, is Marcus stupid?" asked Ethan. "Can we visit him when he goes to prison?"

Lowering Evan to the floor, Beanie rose and went to the kitchen drawer for the ice cream scooper. "Marcus made a mistake."

"What kind of mistake?"

"Mistake!" sang Evan, commencing his laps around the island. "Mistake!"

"Well, a mistake that got him in trouble," said Beanie, returning to the island.

"What kind of trouble?" asked Ethan, concern in his brown eyes.

"Trouble you don't have to worry about," said Beanie, anxious to change the subject. "Now, do you want chocolate syrup, sprinkles, or both?"

"Sprinkles!" said Evan, crawling around Beanie's feet. "Sprinkles!"

Ethan said, "I want both Daddy!"

"Then both you'll get," said Beanie, though he knew his wife might object to the excess sugar. Nevertheless, he was happy to get his four-year-old away from thoughts about the type of trouble that might land you in prison.

"And can we have whipped cream, too, Daddy?" asked Ethan. "Please!"

"Please, Daddy, whip cream!" Little Evan jumped up and down. "Whip cream!"

Laughing, Beanie said, "Okay, sure, you can have—"

A buzzing in the pocket of his cargo shorts startled Beanie for a second, or so before he realized his cell phone was going off.

"Hold on, guys," he said, removing the phone. "This might be Mommy."

"Hi Mommy!" shouted Ethan.

"Mommy!" echoed Evan. "Mommy!"

Beanie checked the Caller-ID.

It wasn't his wife. He didn't recognize the number but answered anyway. "Roland Bean."

"Hey, yeah, this is PJ … Marcus's friend. We met the other day—"

"Oh, yes, hi …" said Beanie.

"Hi Mommy!" said Ethan. "We miss you, Mommy!"

"I want Mommy!" said Evan, reaching his hands up toward Beanie. "Mommy! Mommy!"

"Guys, it's not Mommy," said Beanie. "Daddy needs to take this call, okay?"

"Okay, Daddy!" said Ethan. "Be quiet, Evan! Daddy needs to talk on the phone!"

Beanie stepped over to the short hallway that led into the kitchen where he could both hear PJ and keep an eye on the boys.

"Sorry about that," said Beanie. "How can I help you?"

"Actually, I might be able to help you," said PJ. "Well, help Marcus …"

"I'm listening," said Beanie.

"The maid who works for Fred Zachary told me she might have some information that the police should know," said PJ.

"Has she told the police this information?" asked Beanie, snapping his fingers at Ethan, who was about to climb on top of the island. "Get down. Now."

"But Daddy the ice cream is going to melt," said Ethan.

Through gritted teeth, Beanie whispered, "Get down. Do as Daddy says! Do you understand?"

Pouting, Ethan crossed his arms but stayed on the stool.

"That's your kids acting up?" asked PJ, a casual familiarness in his tone.

Beanie sighed. "Unfortunately. Sorry."

"No worries, man," said PJ. "I got a little girl. She's a handful, so I definitely understand. Anyway, like I said, the Zachary maid has information."

"Has she gone to the cops?"

"She's afraid to," said PJ. "And I don't blame her. She's a maid. She's got information about one of these rich guys which could implicate him in the murder of another employee. Who are the police going to believe? Especially when she can't really prove what she knows. It would come down to her word against Mr. Zachary's."

"Is the maid's name Mabel?"

"That's right," said PJ. "You know her?"

Remembering the petite woman who cowered in Fred Zachary's belligerent presence, Beanie said, "I met her once. What information does she have?"

"I'm not sure," said PJ. "All I know is that, whatever she knows, she wants to tell someone in case something bad happens to her."

30

At eight in the morning, the breakroom at the administration building was hushed, frosty from the A/C, and mostly empty.

With his cup of coffee, Beanie sat at a table in the far corner of the cavernous room. Across from him, in her coral-colored dress, Mabel Estes glanced furtively from Beanie to Joshua, who sat to the right of her.

Following his conversation with PJ last night, and after he scooped generous helpings of ice cream into bowls for the boys, Beanie called Joshua and relayed the information. PJ had promised to facilitate the meeting with Mabel Estes. Joshua agreed to be there.

Earlier this morning, around six a.m., Beanie received a text from the janitor.

PJ
Mabel will be waiting for you in the admin breakroom @ 8.

Beanie said, "Mrs. Estes, first of all, Joshua and I would like to thank you for agreeing to talk to us."

"There's nothing to thank me for," said the housekeeper, glancing over her shoulder. "It wasn't my idea to talk to you."

"Whose idea was it?" asked Joshua.

"Paul Jones. PJ," she said. "After I told him that I had information about what happened to Pablo Lima, but I couldn't go to the police, he said he would help me. I didn't know he wanted me to talk to some reporters. I don't want my name in the papers. I'll lose my job, for sure."

"Because management told staff not to speak to the media," said Beanie.

Nodding, Mabel said, "I don't even think I should be seen talking to you. People probably know who you are."

"Well, we could meet somewhere else at a later time," said Joshua.

"Would you prefer that?" asked Beanie.

The housekeeper sighed. "This is a small island. People are nosey and they gossip. There's nowhere we could go where somebody wouldn't see us."

"Okay, then," said Joshua. "Let's make this as quick as possible since we're pretty much the only people here."

Beanie asked, "What information do you have about the case?"

"A few days after Pablo Lima died," began the housekeeper, her voice lowered, "I heard Mr. and Mrs. Zachary arguing about Pablo."

"Why were they arguing about Pablo?" asked Joshua.

"Mrs. Zachary was in the breakfast nook having coffee with a friend," said Mabel. "They were talking about how horrible it was that Pablo had been killed. And then her friend left. And then Mr. Zachary came into the breakfast nook and started saying that Mrs. Zachary was upset about Pablo because ... "

"Because?" Beanie prompted.

Lips pursed, Mabel shook her head. "I don't like to repeat vile things, but ... he said that Mrs. Zachary was only sad about Pablo being dead because she couldn't be with him anymore."

"Couldn't be with him?" asked Joshua.

Mabel looked down. "Intimately."

"And what did Mrs. Zachary say?" Beanie asked.

"She started cursing at Mr. Zachary," said Mabel. "And he cursed back at her. From what I could tell, Mr. Zachary was accusing Mrs. Zachary of having an affair with Pablo Lima."

Beanie scratched his chin and glanced at Joshua. The former intern seemed as confounded as Beanie felt. He wasn't sure what to think about the relationship between Mrs. Zachary and Pablo Lima. They'd gotten so many conflicting accounts.

"Anyway," continued Mabel. "Then Mrs. Zachary said something like, is that why you killed him?"

"Wait. What?" asked Joshua, frowning.

Beanie asked, "Are you saying that you heard Mrs. Zachary ask Mr. Zachary if he killed Pablo Lima?"

With a shuddering breath, the housekeeper nodded. "And then Mr. Zachary told her …"

"Told her what?" asked Joshua, his gaze intense as he leaned over the table.

Her eyes suddenly bright with unshed tears, Mabel said, "He told her that she better keep her mouth shut, or she would end up just like him …"

31

"What Mabel Estes told you and Joshua this morning proves that Fred Zachary killed Pablo Lima," said Noelle.

Removing his sunglasses, Beanie looked at his wife, stretched out on the chaise next to him.

All he wanted was to waste the afternoon away lounging on the terrace overlooking the pool at the Bronson villa. He'd assumed Noelle wanted to do the same since the boys were napping under the watchful eye of a resort nanny. The studious, pleasant young woman had arrived when Beanie, Noelle, and the kids returned from their family jaunt to one of the gorgeous, pristine black sand beaches the Aerie Islands was known for.

But, instead of enjoying the rest of their day, Noelle wanted to discuss Pablo Lima.

Sighing, Beanie asked, "What makes you say that?"

"You told me that Mabel said Fred Zachary threatened his wife when she accused him of killing Pablo," said Noelle. "He didn't deny it. If he hadn't killed Pablo, then he would have denied it."

"True, but ..."

"But what?" demanded his wife. "You told me Joshua thinks the same thing."

"But what Mabel Estes told us is akin to hearsay," said Beanie. "It could easily be dismissed as gossip. Or an outright lie."

"Why would Mabel Estes lie?"

"Well, for one, I'm sure she doesn't like Fred Zachary," said Beanie. "He's pretty much a tyrant to her, which I witnessed myself. Maybe she wants to get him in trouble."

"Well, if she thinks no one will believe her," said Noelle, "then why make up a lie that no one will believe? How does that get Fred Zachary in trouble? Lying is more of a risk to her."

"I'm not accusing her of lying—"

"You sound like you are," said Noelle.

Beanie shook his head. "I'm just trying to stay objective. I don't want to jump to conclusions. Or get anyone's hopes up for no reason, you know?"

"Okay, fine," said his wife. "Are you at least going to tell the police?"

"Joshua is handling that," said Beanie. "His girlfriend, Friday, is the chief detective's administrative assistant."

"Hopefully, the police will talk to Fred Zachary and his wife," said Noelle. "And hopefully the wife will tell the truth and won't be afraid that her husband will kill her for being honest."

"Hopefully," agreed Beanie, slipping his sunglasses back on.

"And what about Fred's other wives," said Noelle. "Is Joshua going to tell the cops about their suspicious deaths?"

Beanie was suddenly regretting telling Noelle about the progress of his investigations. His wife was turning into an amateur sleuth.

"Babe, I'm sure Joshua will tell the police everything they need to know," assured Beanie.

"Roland, I think you should make sure," said Noelle. "The police have to be aware of everything you and Joshua have found out. It is imperative. Marcus is fighting for his freedom."

Beanie removed his glasses again. "I know what's at stake, Elle. And I am trying to help Marcus, but he hasn't made it easy. He wasn't honest with me—"

"Because he was scared, Roland," said Noelle. "But now he's come clean—"

"Has he?"

Noelle frowned, offense in her gaze. "How can you ask that?"

Beanie sat up, swung his legs over the side of the chaise, and faced his wife. "How do we know what Marcus put in that scotch."

"He told us what he put in the scotch," said Noelle. "Cannabis powder. And, no, he shouldn't have done it, but I happen to know—because I am a pharmacist—that the combination of the cannabis powder and the scotch would not be lethal."

"What I mean is, what if it wasn't cannabis powder?"

"Well, it wasn't antifreeze," Noelle shot back.

"Elle, we don't know what—"

Beanie's phone, lying on the ground beneath the lounge, rang. Thankful for the interruption, he grabbed the phone and looked at the Caller-ID.

"Who is it?" asked Noelle.

"Joshua," said Beanie, and then answered. "Hey, what's going on?"

"Friday told me the cops got the tests back on the poison that killed Pablo Lima," said Joshua.

A spike of adrenaline shot through Beanie. "Was it antifreeze?"

"Not even close," said the former intern. "It was black mamba snake venom ..."

32

"Noelle and I had breakfast with Carmen, and Marcus," said Beanie, coffee cup in hand as he sat in the guest chair in Joshua's spacious cubicle. "Apparently, his lawyer spoke with them last night about the black mamba venom. Carmen is hoping Marcus will be cleared because he doesn't even know what black mamba venom is so how could he have obtained the venom and used it to kill Pablo Lima."

Swiveling from his computer to face Beanie, Joshua nodded. "I think he's telling the truth."

Beanie took a sip of coffee and sighed. "For the first time, I think he's being honest, too."

"Friday said the forensics team is confident, a hundred percent sure that the venom killed Pablo," said Joshua. "So, they need to prove that Marcus had access to the black mamba venom, but the detectives are starting to think they need to look for other suspects."

"I doubt the police will connect Marcus to the venom," said Beanie. "I can't even have imagined how he would have gotten it."

Joshua said, "Someone would have had to have given it to him."

Beanie asked, "But who? I doubt Marcus knows someone with access to black mamba venom."

"Actually, he does," said Joshua, leaning back in his chair. "Sasha Hidalgo."

Confused, Beanie shook his head. "What?"

"When Fri told me about the black mamba venom," said Joshua, "it sparked a memory. So I went looking through my notes. Remember when we went to the Aerie Island Zoo to question Sasha Hidalgo? She didn't really want to talk to us. Said she had to get back to work. You remember what she was doing?"

"Oh my God," said Beanie, remembering. "She was going to milk a black mamba for its venom."

"Marcus and Sasha are friends," said Joshua. "She could have given him the venom."

"Or Sasha could have put the venom in the scotch," said Beanie.

"I was thinking that," admitted Joshua. "Remember, PJ accused Sasha of killing Pablo Lima because she was jealous about him hooking up with other girls."

"Sasha dismissed PJ's accusations," recalled Beanie.

"But she didn't deny threatening to kill Pablo," said Joshua. "Although she claimed it was an empty threat she never planned to carry out. Just an angry expression."

"And then she pointed the finger at Fred Zachary," said Beanie. "She was the first person to bring up the alleged affair between Pablo and Mrs. Zachary."

"Which Marcus denied," said Joshua. "But, then according to Mabel Estes, the maid, the Zacharys argued about Mrs. Zachary having an affair with Pablo."

"And then Mr. Zachary told his wife to stay quiet or she would end up like Pablo," said Beanie.

"But if Mr. Zachary did kill Pablo then we still have the question of how he got the black mamba venom," said Joshua.

"He's a wealthy guy," said Beanie, taking another sip of coffee. "He could have paid someone for it. Maybe Sasha. Who knows?"

Joshua shook his head. "I don't think so. Sasha accused Fred Zachary of killing Pablo. If she had given him the venom, wouldn't she be afraid that he would tell the cops she had given it to him, which might make her an accessory?"

"So, if Sasha killed Pablo," began Beanie, "then she points the finger at Fred because she knows about the alleged affair between Mrs. Zachary and Pablo which gives Fred a motive, throwing suspicion onto him and away from herself."

"That's what I think," said Joshua, swiveling back to face his computer. "But here's something I know that makes me more suspicious of Sasha."

"What's that?" asked Beanie, finishing his coffee.

"I started doing a background investigation on Sasha," said Joshua, opening files with the click of his mouse.

"What did you find out?"

"Well, a police report was filed against her last year," said Joshua. "By the Aerie Islands Zoo."

Beanie was floored. "What did she do?"

"Apparently," said Joshua, reading his screen. "The zoo called the cops on her because she got into an altercation with another person on the premises."

"Another person on the premises?" Beanie frowned. "What does that mean? What was the altercation?"

"There aren't any additional notes," said Joshua. "The zoo withdrew the complaint and no charges were filed. But, I'm wondering if that altercation was with Pablo Lima."

Beanie nodded. "He might be the unauthorized person if he showed up in an unauthorized area of the zoo."

"I found someone who might be willing to talk to us about the incident," said Joshua. "His name is Trent Miller. He was janitor at the zoo, but he doesn't work there anymore. He's got a stall at the flea market near Rudolph Beach."

Standing, Beanie said, "Well, let's see if he's willing to talk to us ..."

33

Under a canopy of mature banana trees decorated with colorful pennant flags stretched between the trunks, Beanie and Joshua traversed hardpacked white sand, maneuvering among hundreds of pedestrians. Under the blazing sun, the warm sea breeze swirled, mixing with the jaunty calypso music from a nearby live band.

A collection of retail and food stalls positioned in front of the tree line, the Rudolph Beach Market was a popular tourist destination showcasing local products, from art and clothing to indigenous crafts and herbal medicines.

Trent Miller, the former zoo janitor, had a stall selling candles and aromatherapy oils.

Map in hand, Joshua led the way through the maze of stalls. The crowd was thick, and the narrow pathways forced traffic into a single line at times. The kaleidoscope of sights, sounds, and smells contributed to an atmosphere that was both lively and claustrophobic.

The former zoo employee was busy with a cluster of customers when Beanie and Joshua finally found his stall, a small space constructed of four thin metal poles with a faded blue tarp overhead. Most of the wares, candles, oils, and lotions in various sizes and colors were displayed on top of overturned wooden crates. The setup was rudimentary, and a tad low rent, but the area smelled amazing. A calming, musky, spicy fragrance that enticed people to stop and explore.

As he sniffed a light green candle, trying to determine the scent, Beanie checked out Trent Miller.

Tall and rangy with lean muscles, he had stringy sun-bleached hair and a par-boiled complexion that was indicative of exposure to harsh rays without the proper sunscreen.

Moments later, when the customers left, Beanie alerted Joshua.

"Mr. Miller …" said Joshua, walking to the makeshift checkout counter—a waist-high metal file cabinet with an office calculator on top of it. "I'm Joshua Howard from the *Aerie Observer*. I called this morning—"

"You got questions about Sasha?" asked Trent, sneering, and rolling his eyes.

"Right," said Joshua.

"All I can tell you is that I got this stall because of Sasha Hidalgo," said Trent.

"Sasha helped you get the stall?" asked Beanie.

Trent scoffed. "Sasha got me fired from my job at the zoo. So, I ended up doing this. Selling candles and lotions that my mom makes."

"How did she get you fired?" asked Joshua.

"Sasha stole my employee badge and used it to enter the zoo after hours," said Trent.

"Why would she do that?" asked Beanie.

"So, she could steal vials of black mamba venom from the milking lab," said Trent.

Joshua asked, "When was this?"

"About a year ago," said Trent.

"A year," said Beanie, wondering about the efficacy of venom after so long. Could it still be potent enough to kill? If so, was it possible that Sasha Hidalgo could have spiked the poisoned scotch with venom she'd stolen last year? But why would she wait so long to use the venom?

Beanie stopped his train of thought.

He cautioned himself not to speculate or jump to conclusions without the complete facts. After all, Trent's account would have to be verified. Was the ex-employee telling the truth? Or did he have some sort of ax to grind?

"Me and Sasha had gone out drinking one Friday after work," said Trent. "I think she put something in my rum because, after two drinks, I was stumbling and slurring. She drove my car back to my place. The last thing I remember is she helped me get into bed and said she would sleep on my couch and I could drive her home in the morning. Which I did, even though I had the worst hangover of my life."

"So how did you find out that she stole the venom?" asked Beanie.

"Well, Monday morning, I show up to work and the big bosses and the head of security want to talk to me," Trent said. "They start questioning me about some missing vials of snake venom. I have no idea what they are talking about, of course. They tell me that the exterior surveillance cameras caught my car entering through the employee gate. They say my badge was used to get into the milking lab. I deny everything. I tell them I was drunk Friday night, out like a light, and I have an alibi, Sasha can back up my story."

"Did she?" Joshua asked.

Scowling, Trent said, "They question Sasha. She admits that we went out Friday night but she says I drove myself home. She has no idea of my whereabouts after I left the bar."

"Do you have proof that Sasha stole the vials?" asked Beanie.

"No, unfortunately," said Trent. "There are no surveillance cameras in the hepatology building. But, since my badge was used, it looked like I had entered the lab. That's what my boss and security believed. So, they fired me."

"But they couldn't really prove that you took the vials, either," Joshua pointed out.

"Their suspicions of me was enough for them to terminate my employment," said Trent.

"Did you tell them your suspicions about Sasha?" Beanie asked.

"Yeah, but my boss didn't want to hear a bad word about her," sneered Trent. "That old, perverted goat has a crush on her. Even if he did suspect Sasha, he wouldn't have fired her. He let her get away with everything. He didn't even write her up when she slapped Mrs. Zachary."

"Slapped Mrs. Zachary?" asked Joshua.

Beanie asked, "Is that why the zoo filed a complaint against her?"

Nodding, Trent said, "Sasha should have gone to jail for assaulting that poor woman but the zoo didn't pursue charges. And it's crazy because Mrs. Zachary is a patron of the zoo. But I heard that her husband, also a big contributor, told the zoo to drop the complaint because he didn't want the publicity."

"And the husband Fred Zachary?" asked Joshua.

"Right," said Trent.

Beanie asked, "Why did Sasha slap Mrs. Zachary?"

"Sasha confronted Mrs. Zachary at one of the luncheons the zoo hosts throughout the year for its patrons and contributors," said Trent.

"Confronted Mrs. Zachary about what?" asked Joshua.

"I wasn't there. It happened a few months ago," said Trent. "But what I heard was that Sasha accused Mrs. Zachary of fooling around with her boyfriend."

"Her boyfriend?" asked Joshua.

"The lifeguard who was killed," said Trent. "Pablo Lima."

34

"I don't have any statement about that unfortunate incident," said Mrs. Fred Zachary. "I do not wish to revisit that horrid mortification."

Beanie nodded, hoping his face reflected an appropriate amount of sympathy, even though he didn't really feel sorry for the woman, who appeared chic and regal, lounging on a chaise on the terrace of her villa.

After the revelation from Trent Miller, Beanie and Joshua decided that a visit to Fred Zachary's wife was in order. The bombshell accusation about Sasha Hidalgo stealing black mamba venom was not the only information that needed to be thoroughly vetted. Concerning the division of labor, Beanie figured he should try to talk to Mrs. Zachary while Joshua would look into the stolen venom.

As he drove the golf cart to the Zachary villa, Beanie had started to feel, maybe for the first time, that he might be able to clear Marcus's name. If Joshua could find evidence that showed Sasha as the venom thief, and if Beanie could solidify the young woman's motive—jealous romantic rivalry—then perhaps the cops would consider a more probable suspect.

Beanie had taken a chance that Mrs. Zachary would be home, and if so, that she would talk to him.

So far, he'd batted a thousand.

But now, he'd suffered his first swing and miss.

Clearing his throat, Beanie said, "I know it might be difficult to talk about, but—"

"Difficult to talk about?" Mrs. Zachary scoffed. "I have never been so embarrassed in my life. People are still gossiping about it. I was made a fool of, and for what? A ridiculous little trollop suffering paranoid delusions?"

"Paranoid delusions?"

Mrs. Zachary pursed her lips in disgust. "She was ranting like a lunatic, accusing me of having an affair with the lifeguard who was killed."

"Pablo Lima," supplied Beanie.

"She actually threatened to kill me," said Mrs. Zachary, her voice brimming with indignant outrage. "I wanted her fired. I wanted her in jail for attempted murder. Did either one of those things happen? No. And do you want to know why Sasha Hidalgo wasn't fired or arrested?"

"Your husband convinced the zoo to drop the complaint against Sasha?"

Shaking her head, Mrs. Zachary said, "The zoo's board of directors deferred to Fred's wishes because he's a very important donor. But you want to know what's ironic about that? Fred's contributions are made with my money."

"Fred doesn't have his own money?"

"As it turns out," she said, "He doesn't. His first two wives were fairly wealthy and he got his dirty hands on their fortunes after they died. But I have more money than the two of them put together. Which Fred was aware of when he courted me. I, unfortunately, didn't know that he'd blown through the millions he'd inherited as a widower. He presented himself as financially independent and stable. But that wasn't the case."

"When did you find out he was broke?"

"While we were dating," she said.

"And you still married him?"

"I was in love with him," she said, somewhat wistful as she stared toward the shimmering water. "I guess I still am, even though I shouldn't be but the heart wants what it wants, right?"

"I suppose so," agreed Beanie.

"But love is not the same as trust," she said. "Fred wanted to marry me, and I knew he loved me, but my bank account was also attractive to him. I told him we couldn't get married unless he signed a prenup which included a clause stating that if I learned that he was cheating on me, I would divorce him and he would get nothing. And, to make things fair, if he caught me cheating, he could divorce me, and I would give him ten million dollars."

"Interesting," said Beanie.

"Which is why Fred has taken to periodically accusing me of cheating," said Mrs. Zachary. "After fifteen years of marriage, he's no longer interested in preserving our union."

"Let me guess," said Beanie. "He wants the ten million."

Mrs. Zachary's laugh lacked mirth. "He won't get it."

"Because you're not cheating on him," said Beanie.

"Because Fred is projecting."

"Projecting?"

"You know how they say that when someone accuses you of cheating it's often because they're cheating?"

Beanie scratched his chin. "I've heard that."

"Yes, well, when I divorce Fred, he's not going to get a dime."

"You can prove that Fred has cheated on you?" asked Beanie.

"That's not all I can prove," said Mrs. Zachary.

"What do you mean?"

"I believe that Fred killed Pablo Lima."

Beanie recalled Mabel Estes's story but decided not to bring it up. "Why do you think that?"

"Pablo Lima knew that Fred was cheating on me," said Mrs. Zachary. "He was blackmailing Fred."

35

"I didn't steal any snake venom!" insisted Sasha Hidalgo. "Who told you that?"

"We spoke with Trent Miller," said Joshua.

Sasha let forth a string of curses, then said, "He's a liar. He was accused of stealing the venom and they fired him for it!"

"Trent believes he was fired unjustly," said Beanie. "He says you stole his employee identification badge and used it to enter the zoo after hours and steal the venom."

Sasha laughed out loud. "Are you kidding me?"

"Um … what's going on?"

At the plaintive, uncertain voice behind him, Beanie turned.

Daisy Cox, Sasha's best friend, and roommate, stood under the arched opening that separated the living area of the small apartment from the bedrooms. From her bleary eyes, tousled hair, and the rumbled pajamas she wore, Beanie guessed she'd been sleeping. Sort of surprising. True, it was after nine o'clock in the night, but Beanie didn't think twentysomethings went to bed before midnight.

"Sorry, Daze," said Sasha. "These low-rent, fake news, wanna-be reporters are, once again, accusing me of killing Pablo."

"Why do you think Sasha killed Pablo?" asked Daisy, hugging her arms around her thin frame as she wobbled into the living room.

Joshua said, "If you read my story in the *Aerie Observer*, then you know that Pablo Lima died from ingesting black mamba venom."

"Mamba venom?" Daisy's face crumpled and reddened. "Oh, my God! I didn't know. I didn't read the story."

"Yeah, well, I did," said Sasha. "And now they think I killed Pablo because I had access to black mamba venom, which I did because I work in the herpetology department at the zoo. But I didn't steal any venom. The zoo has policies in place to prevent that kind of theft."

"Policies you might have known how to get around," suggested Joshua.

Sasha rolled her eyes. "Again, I ask, are you kidding me? Listen, Trent lied to you. And you want to know why? Because I wouldn't hook up with him. Yes, we went out drinking the night the mamba venom was stolen. But he started hitting on me. I told him I wasn't interested. He got mad and left. I don't know where he went or what he did after that. Right, Daze?"

Beanie turned to look at Daisy Cox, now sitting on the couch, feet on the cushion, arms wrapped tight around her bony knees.

"Daisy!" barked Sasha.

Flinching violently, Daisy looked up at Sasha. "What?"

Sasha glared at her best friend. "Tell them that I had to call you to pick me up from that bar after Trent abandoned me!"

Her eyes wide and glistening, Daisy nodded. "I had to pick Sasha up. Trent was such a toad. He left her there."

Beanie glanced at Joshua.

The former intern looked skeptical, but said to Sasha, "Trent Miller isn't the only zoo employee I spoke with."

Beanie knew the former intern was about to share the information he'd divulged on the drive to Sasha's apartment after Beanie picked him up from the *Aerie Observer*.

"What are you talking about?" demanded Sasha, flipping a thick column of hair over her shoulder.

"Andy Yates, one of the night guards at the zoo, remembered the stolen venom incident, even though it happened a year ago," said Joshua.

"I don't know Andy Yates," declared Sasha as she pivoted away from them and stomped into the small, galley kitchen. "And if he said he knows me, he's a liar."

Joshua said, "Andy Yates knows that the surveillance photos that captured Trent's car entering the zoo after hours on the night the black mamba venom was stolen also showed that Trent wasn't driving the car."

"Let me guess," said Sasha, loading the dishwasher with dirty dishes stacked high in the kitchen sink. "The video surveillance shows that I was driving the car, right?"

"Actually, the video was a bit grainy," said Joshua. "But it was clearly a woman driving the car. And she had dark brown hair."

"Which proves it wasn't me," said Sasha. "As you can see, I'm a blonde."

Not a natural blonde, Beanie thought but decided not to say, wary that Sasha might toss a food-crusted plate at him.

"You didn't have blonde hair a year ago," said Joshua.

Sasha scowled at the former intern but said nothing as she continued loading dishes.

"Tell me this," said Joshua. "You said you and Pablo hooked up but it didn't mean anything …"

Her dishes loaded, Sasha slammed the door closed. "Because it didn't mean anything."

"If that's the case, then why did you slap Mrs. Zachary and accuse her of messing around with Pablo Lima?" asked Joshua.

"How about I tell you this," said Sasha. "Get out of my apartment!"

36

"What do you think Marcus's chances are?" asked Noelle, rearranging items in her opened suitcase.

Standing on the opposite side of the king-sized bed, folding a T-shirt, Beanie said, "I'd like to say pretty good, but I don't know. Still, I'm hopeful, though."

Exhaling, Noelle nodded and wedged a few souvenirs between several rolled-up sundresses.

As he packed his suitcase, a feeling of melancholy washed over Beanie.

Today was the final day of their vacation. Fourteen days had passed, and now it was time to head back to real life. He wished it had all been fun in the sun but there had been just as much investigation as relaxation. Thankfully, the last two days had been spent exclusively vacationing. He, Noelle, and the boys had enjoyed quality time at several different beaches, sightseeing, shopping, and eating too much. Beanie hadn't thought once about Marcus's case, or the death of Pablo Lima, or doing any investigating or speculating.

After the conversation with Sasha Hidalgo, Beanie and Joshua decided that Joshua would continue with any sleuthing that needed to be done. But, the two agreed that Sasha Hidalgo had most likely killed Pablo.

The fiery, foul-mouthed snake charmer had motive, opportunity, and most importantly, means.

Sasha's violent, unrestrained jealousy over Pablo's cheating led her to kill him, something she seemed to have planned a year in advance. She had access to the black mamba venom and could have easily emptied a vial of the toxin in the bottle of scotch at some time during the wild car ride before the accident.

Joshua had taken the investigative findings to his girlfriend Friday, who'd promised to share them with her boss, the lead detective at the Aerie Islands Police Department.

"I just wish there was conclusive proof connecting Sasha to the venom in the scotch," said Noelle.

"There is," said Beanie, staring at his wife. "Sasha had access to the venom—"

"Yeah, I know that," said Noelle, sighing as she removed a few articles of clothing to make room for more purchases. "Obviously, Sasha stole that venom. But did she put it in the scotch? There's no proof that she did that. And I just wish there was because ..."

"Because ...?" prompted Beanie.

Noelle folded a pair of pajama bottoms into a small square. "Because what if the cops think that Sasha gave the stolen venom to Marcus? Or that Marcus stole the venom from Sasha."

"Babe, if Sasha gave that venom to Marcus, I think she'll tell the cops that," said Beanie. "I don't think she would protect Marcus."

"Unless maybe she would," said Noelle. "Unless maybe they're in some secret relationship."

"Secret relationship? You think that?"

"I don't know. No, not really," admitted Noelle. "I'm just hoping the police will take a critical look at the evidence."

"Listen, the cops are certain that the venom killed Pablo," said Beanie. "And Marcus had no way of getting that venom. Sasha didn't give it to him. He didn't steal it. The important thing is, Marcus fails the means test. Maybe he's got a motive. And yes, he had opportunity. But, still, I think the cops are going to drop the charges."

"And maybe they'll arrest Sasha?" asked Noelle.

Beanie picked up another T-shirt from the pile of clothes next to this suitcase. "I don't know. Maybe. But, the most important thing is that Marcus's name will be cleared. That's what Carmen wanted."

Noelle smiled. "Well, I told her you could do it and you did."

"Yeah, and I felt no pressure whatsoever to fulfill a promise I didn't make," joked Beanie.

"Silly!" Noelle tossed a pair of socks at him.

Beanie ducked, allowing the socks to sail past him.

"But, aren't you curious?" asked Noelle.

"About what?"

"About who really killed Pablo Lima," said Noelle. "I mean, I think it was Sasha, but at one time you thought it was Fred Zachary."

Groaning, Beanie said, "He would still be on my list. But, I think he also fails the means test. How would he get the black mamba venom?"

"I guess it's strange to think of someone committing murder over stolen scotch," said Noelle.

"And you would think that Fred would be upset about Pablo fooling around with his wife," said Beanie, "but I don't think Pablo and Mrs. Zachary were having an affair."

"But I'm sure Fred Zachary wishes they had been," said Noelle. "Then Fred could divorce her and collect ten million dollars."

Beanie shook his head. "That's some marriage, huh?"

"Would you divorce me for ten million dollars?" asked his wife, a hint of mischief in her gaze.

"Babe, I would divorce you for a million dollars," deadpanned Beanie.

Shrieking in fake outrage, Noelle tossed a barrage of clothes at him. "Good thing I don't have a million dollars!"

Laughing, Beanie feinted left and right, trying to dodge the clothes. "Babe, you know I'm kidding!"

"You better be!"

"I'm not divorcing you," said Beanie, gathering up the clothes from the floor. "You are not getting rid of me."

Noelle laughed. "Well, you—"

Beanie's phone rang.

"Ha!" Beanie chuckled, sidestepping to the bed table. "Saved by the bell."

Noelle made a face and continued her packing.

"Hello?" answered Beanie.

"Mr. Roland …" The voice was low and tremulous.

"Yes, this is Roland," said Beanie, trying to discern the whispery tone.

Following a shuddering exhale, the person said, "It's Marcus …"

"Marcus?" Beanie's pulse jumped. "What's going on?"

"Is everything okay?" asked Noelle.

Glancing at his wife, Beanie shrugged.

"Can you come please …" pleaded Marcus.

"Can I come … where?" asked Beanie.

"What is he saying?" demanded Noelle.

"I'm in trouble," Marcus said, sniffing.

"What kind of trouble?" asked Beanie, his heart starting to pound.

"Oh, my God!" Noelle exclaimed.

"Marcus, what's happened?" Beanie asked.

"Sasha …" whimpered Marcus. "She's dead …"

37

Gripping the steering wheel, his heart pounding, Beanie drove the SUV to Sasha Hidalgo's apartment complex.

Dozens of police vehicles and an ambulance were already there, thank goodness. Twenty minutes ago, before hanging up with Marcus, Beanie had told the shell-shocked kid to call 911. He'd promised Marcus that he was on his way. Noelle stayed behind to call Carmen.

A swarm of cops and crime scene techs milled about the parking lot, while residents stood on the perimeter, their expressions grim and shocked as they talked among each other. After finding a parking space, Beanie exited the car. Near the opened door of Sasha's place, Beanie spotted Marcus looking toward two paramedics rolling the dead body on a stretcher toward the ambulance.

Beanie jogged over to Marcus. Carefully, he touched the young man's shoulder. Flinching, Marcus turned to him, confusion, and pain in his haunted gaze.

"How are you doing?" asked Beanie.

Marcus shook his head. "I don't understand. How can Sasha be dead?"

"Did you talk to the police?" asked Beanie.

"They took my statement," Marcus said.

"And what did you tell them?" Beanie asked.

"Sasha was dead …"

Beanie guided Marcus toward a large guava tree, where they could talk in the shade, and somewhat privately, though residents and a few cops kept glancing in their direction.

"Marcus, I want you to start from the beginning," Beanie said. "Why were you at Sasha's apartment?"

"I needed to talk to her," said Marcus. "I had to ask her why she was going to lie on me."

"Lie on you?"

"Sasha was gonna tell the cops I forced her to steal that black mamba venom for me," said Marcus, his eyes wild, his voice rising with incredulity. "And that I used it to kill Pablo, but this is not true! I didn't even know Sasha could get snake venom! I knew she worked at the zoo with snakes, but I didn't know what she did! I didn't use that venom to kill Pablo and I wanted Sasha to tell me why she was gonna lie on me!"

"Okay, okay …" said Beanie, placing his hands on Marcus's shoulders. "Calm down, okay."

"I didn't ask Sasha to steal venom for me," insisted Marcus.

"Listen, Marcus, I believe you," said Beanie. "But, why did you think Sasha was going to lie to the cops about you? Did she tell you—"

"Daisy told me," said Marcus. "Thank God, she did! Sasha was gonna blindside me. Throw me under the bus! And why? Because she probably killed Pablo."

Confused, Beanie asked, "Daisy told you?"

Nodding, Marcus said, "We saw each other in the breakroom this morning. Daisy said she had something to tell me. And then she told me what Sasha was planning to do. She said Sasha was going to talk to the cops around ten o'clock. It was eight something when Daisy told me. So, I took my first break at nine forty-five so I could get over here before Sasha left."

"And did you talk to Sasha?"

"No, she was dead!" Marcus sighed, threw up his hands, and turned from Beanie, stumbling toward the tree trunk.

Beanie approached him. "She was dead in the apartment?"

Facing the tree trunk, Marcus nodded.

"How did you get in the apartment?"

"The door was open," said Marcus. "Like, half open. Like, somebody had left without closing it, you know?"

Beanie had encountered several half-opened doors in his career, and against his better judgment, he'd entered more than a few.

"So you went inside?"

Marcus faced Beanie. "I wasn't even thinking that it was kind of weird. All I could focus on was stopping Sasha from going to the cops and lying on me."

Beanie frowned. "Did you tell the police that?"

"Yeah, I did," said Marcus, dropping his head. "And I know it makes me look bad. And I know the cops probably don't believe the door was open when I got here. I know they think I killed Sasha because she was going to give a statement about me to the police, but that's not true. She was dead when I got here."

"And where did you find the body?"

"In her bedroom," said Marcus. "She was lying in the bed, covered in blood. I didn't know what to do. That's when I called you and—"

"Marcus! Marcus!"

Beanie glanced toward the anguished cries.

Carmen Taylor ran toward them, arms outstretched. Noelle followed Carmen, her expression worried as she walked at a brisk pace.

"Mom!" Marcus hurried to meet Carmen.

Mother and son met, wrapping their arms around each other. As Marcus broke down sobbing, Carmen cried and comforted him.

"Oh my God," whispered Noelle as she embraced Beanie. "I can't believe this is happening."

Rubbing Noelle's back, Beanie said, "Neither can I…"

Stepping back to look up at him, Noelle asked, "Did you talk to Marcus? Did he … kill Sasha?"

Beanie shook his head. "Marcus didn't kill Sasha. But somebody did. And I'm going to find out who it was…"

38

"Sasha Hidalgo was stabbed to death," said Joshua.

Beanie shuddered, then took a sip of his coffee.

He should have been drinking it at his tiny desk in his tiny cubicle at the *Palmchat Gazette*, in St. Killian, now that his vacation was officially over. But he was still in the Aerie Islands. Still trying to get to the bottom of who was responsible for the death of Pablo Lima. And Sasha Hidalgo.

Yesterday evening, Beanie waved to Noelle and the boys as they boarded the plane back home. He'd wanted to be with them, but his wife suggested that he call his editor and explain Marcus's predicament. His boss, Vivian Thomas-Bronson, a former foreign war correspondent, didn't agree that a young resort employee accused of killing his coworker was compelling enough to warrant Beanie staying in the Aerie Islands. However, he'd been able to convince her of the sinister and subtle components of the story.

Pablo Lima had been a thief and a grifter with many possible enemies, including Fred Zachary, a man who'd been willing to pay to have Lima hurt. Zachary's past as a possible black widower who might have poisoned two former wives for money was lurid enough to entice readers. Lima's alleged girlfriend, who'd had access to the venom that killed him, had been a viable potential suspect until she was murdered.

Vivian agreed to give him one week to wrap up the investigation. His wife had been relieved by Vivian's decision, as she wanted Beanie to make sure Marcus didn't end up behind bars for something he hadn't done. Knowing his wife's empathy toward the falsely accused, Beanie agreed to do his best, but again offered no promises.

"They have any evidence?" asked Beanie.

Swiveling from his computer to face Beanie, Joshua said, "Friday told me that a knife was found under Sasha's bed. They think it's the murder weapon and they're processing it. They collected trace evidence, hairs, and stuff, but a lot of people went in and out of that apartment, so they expect to find all sorts of DNA. What they want is prints and, hopefully, DNA from the knife."

After another sip of coffee, Beanie asked the question he'd been avoiding since he'd arrived at the *Aerie Observer* twenty minutes ago. "And suspects?"

Joshua shook his head. "Fri says they are looking at Marcus."

Beanie sighed. "I was afraid of that."

"As soon as he told the cops that he went to Sasha's apartment to talk to her about trying to frame him," said Joshua, "he gave himself a motive."

"I was afraid of that, too."

"Didn't help that the detectives don't buy his story about Sasha's front door being ajar," said Joshua. "Fri says they want to tie Marcus to the murder weapon. They want to find his DNA on the knife."

"Let's hope they don't," said Beanie.

Joshua said, "Well, let's also hope the cops don't believe what Daisy told them."

Beanie frowned. "What do you mean?"

"Apparently, Daisy told the cops that Marcus killed Pablo."

39

"I don't have time to talk right now, okay?" snapped Daisy Cox, standing on the porch of her aunt's home, where she was staying until the police allowed her to return to the apartment she'd shared with Sasha Hidalgo.

Friday had informed Joshua of Daisy's temporary residence, which the young woman had reported to the police after giving her statement. After learning what Daisy had told the cops about Marcus, Beanie decided another interview was warranted.

"Can you just give us a few minutes?" asked Joshua.

"It's kind of important," said Beanie, staring at the young woman.

Averting her eyes, Daisy folded her arms across her chest. "I don't have a few minutes. I have somewhere to be."

Or, someone to see, wondered Beanie. But, he said, "We just need to confirm something that you told the police."

"Is this about Marcus killing Pablo?" Daisy sneered.

"Why did you tell the police that?" asked Joshua.

"Because it's true," snipped Daisy. "I was tired of lying to the cops for him. And after he killed Sasha—"

"You think Marcus killed Sasha?" interjected Beanie.

Eyes flashing, Daisy said "I know he did. Because Sasha was tired of lying to the cops, too. She was going to tell the police the truth."

"Which was?" prompted Beanie, wanting to hear the story from Daisy's point of view.

Rubbing her arms, Daisy said, "Sasha was going to tell the police that Marcus killed Pablo. He forced Sasha to steal venom from the milking lab so he could use it to kill Pablo. He put it in the scotch. I saw him do it."

"When?" asked Joshua.

"When we were in Sasha's car the day Pablo crashed it," said Daisy. "Me and Marcus were in the backseat. Pablo was drinking scotch straight from the bottle like he normally did. So, Marcus asked Pablo to give him a drink. But Marcus didn't take a drink. Instead, he pulled a vial from his pocket, unscrewed it, and poured the contents into the scotch."

"He did this in front of you?"

Nodding, Daisy said, "He leaned over and whispered that it was some new cannabis oil he'd bought. And then he gave the bottle back to Pablo."

"And you didn't tell Pablo that Marcus had added cannabis oil to the scotch?" asked Beanie.

"I didn't care," snipped Daisy, scowling at him. "All the two of them ever did was drink too much and do drugs so what did it matter to me what Marcus put in that bottle."

"When did Sasha steal the mamba venom?" Joshua asked.

"Last year," said Daisy.

"Marcus forced Sasha to steal venom a year ago?" asked Joshua.

"No, Sasha stole the venom for Pablo," said Daisy. "He wanted to sell it."

"And did Pablo sell it?" Beanie asked.

Shrugging, Daisy said, "Some of it. But not all of it."

"And Sasha kept the venom Pablo wasn't able to sell?" asked Joshua.

"She must have, right?" Daisy said. "Otherwise, she wouldn't have given it to Marcus."

"What did Sasha think Marcus was going to do with the venom?" Beanie asked.

"I don't know," Daisy said. "Maybe she thought he would try to sell it. Look, I have to go, okay? I don't want to be late."

"Late for what?" asked Joshua.

"None of your business," growled Daisy.

Beanie said, "Daisy—"

The young woman turned from them without a word, and went back into her aunt's home, slamming the door behind her.

"Interesting," remarked Joshua. "You believe her?"

As they turned, and walked down the stairs and off the porch, Beanie shook his head. "Not at all. I mean, how did she know it was mamba venom in the vial she claims she saw Marcus remove from his pocket."

"I think she's lying, too," said Joshua. "Notice how, at first, she said that Marcus forced Sasha to steal the venom. Then she says Sasha stole the venom so Pablo could sell it, and then later gave the unsold venom to Marcus."

"Yeah, her story doesn't make sense," said Beanie, using the key fob to unlock the SUV as they approached the vehicle. "She wasn't telling us the truth."

"And don't forget," said Joshua, as he opened the passenger door, "Daisy admitted to lying to the police before. She probably lied to them again."

Inside the SUV, Beanie started the car. "Question is, why is Daisy lying? That's what we need to find out."

40

"Marcus is being set up," said PJ, slouching in the guest chair in Joshua's spacious cubicle. "There's no way Marcus killed Pablo. Or Sasha."

Standing in the doorway of the cube, Beanie regarded the young janitor. He seemed frustrated and worried, which was probably why he'd contacted Joshua and requested to speak with him. Beanie had been having a late lunch when the former intern texted him.

PJ wants to talk. He's coming to the paper. Figured you might want to join us.

Curious as to what the young man had to say, Beanie texted back that he was on his way.

Joshua said, "Daisy told the police—"

"Daisy is lying," said PJ.

"Why do you think she would lie to the police and tell them Marcus killed two people?" asked Beanie.

PJ shook his head. "Okay, maybe she's not lying. Maybe she doesn't know she's lying, you know? Maybe she thinks she knows the truth, but she really doesn't."

Joshua frowned. "Daisy said she saw Marcus put mamba venom in the bottle of scotch that Pablo drank from."

"See, that's what I mean," said PJ, sitting forward, his gaze intense. "How does Daisy know that it was venom in the vial?"

Beanie nodded. "I was wondering that, too. But I started to think, well, Daisy knew Sasha had stolen the venom last year so Pablo could sell it. Maybe Daisy recognized the vial of venom."

Joshua said, "And then she also said that Sasha told her Marcus wanted the venom so he could kill Pablo."

"Look, I don't know what Daisy's deal is," said PJ. "I don't really have nothing to do with her. She's kinda weird. And nothing she said can be proved. How do we know that Sasha told her that Marcus asked for the venom to kill Pablo?"

Beanie said, "Still, if Daisy is lying—and to be honest, I didn't believe her story—then why?"

PJ said, "Listen, I think you need to focus on Fred Zachary. Pablo was blackmailing Fred Zachary."

Beanie thought back to what Mrs. Zachary had told him. *Pablo Lima knew that Fred was cheating on me. He was blackmailing Fred.*

"So Fred does have a good motive," said Beanie, relating the details of his conversation with Mrs. Zachary, which he'd already shared with Joshua.

PJ said, "Well, if Pablo knew Fred Zachary was cheating on his wife, then I think Fred killed Pablo."

The former intern frowned. "But how would Fred have gotten snake venom? And how and when could he have put the venom in the bottle of scotch?"

Beanie said, "Pablo was stealing Fred's scotch. Maybe he spiked all the bottles, hoping that Pablo would take one."

"I'll bet that's what he did," said PJ.

Joshua disagreed. "Yeah, but that's too risky. If Fred did that, he would be assuming that, one, Pablo would drink the scotch and not just sell it, and two, that Pablo wouldn't share the scotch with anyone else. For all Fred knew, Pablo, Sasha, Daisy, and Marcus could have swigged from the bottle. And then Fred kills four people."

"That's true," said Beanie, rubbing his jaw. "And from what Simba told us, Fred wanted Pablo beat up. I think he wanted to scare Pablo so that Pablo would stop blackmailing him."

PJ said, "What if Fred Zachary got someone to put the venom in the scotch for him?"

Joshua asked, "Someone like who?"

Shrugging, PJ said, "Someone who was in the car with Pablo the day he died."

41

"No one is to know you got this from me," said Mabel Estes, pushing several documents, folded in thirds, across the table toward Beanie.

At seven in the morning, the employee breakroom at the Aerie Island Resort Spa was hushed and practically deserted. Beanie had agreed to meet Mable Estes there after she'd called him late last night. She'd spoken to PJ, who'd told her he believed Fred Zachary had killed Pablo. She agreed and felt she had proof that could be taken to the police.

"What is this?"

"Letters from Pablo to Fred Zachary," said Mable. "Pablo paid me to give the letters to Mr. Zachary. I told him they had come with the mail."

"How did you get the letters back?"

"Mr. Zachary read them and threw them in the trash," said Mabel. "I found them when I was cleaning his study. I took them out and kept them. I don't know why. Something told me to do it and I'm glad I did."

Beanie opened the first letter and read it.

I know you are cheating on your wife and I have proof

Mabel Estes said, "I think the police should see that …"

"I agree with Mabel Estes," said Joshua, staring at the letters the housekeeper had given Beanie an hour ago.

Sitting in the guest chair in Joshua's cube, Beanie said, "Can you give the letters to Friday?"

Joshua nodded. "You know, maybe PJ was right."

"About what?"

"Maybe Fred Zachary got someone to put venom in the scotch," said Joshua. "Someone named Sasha Hidalgo."

"Why would Sasha do that?" asked Beanie, curious to hear the former intern's theories.

Joshua said, "Sasha attacked Mrs. Zachary when she thought the woman was having an affair with Pablo. Despite what Sasha wanted people to believe, I think she was crazy about Pablo."

"You're probably right," said Beanie.

"And Pablo made Sasha crazy when he hooked up with other girls," said Joshua. "So I'm thinking that once Fred realized he couldn't get the exiled PC-5 guy to beat up Pablo, he went to Sasha and plotted to poison Pablo with the snake venom, which I am sure he knew Sasha had access to because he's a zoo patron."

"He knew Sasha worked in the milking lab," said Beanie.

Joshua continued, "And Fred stopped the zoo from pressing charges against Sasha. Maybe Fred felt that Sasha owed him. He made sure she didn't end up in jail."

"You really think Sasha wanted Pablo dead?" asked Beanie.

Joshua shook his head. "Not really. And I don't think Fred wanted him dead, either. Remember, Fred wanted Pablo beat up. Taught a lesson."

"So you think Fred and Sasha wanted to make Pablo sick?"

"Like you said yesterday," said Joshua, "Fred just wanted Pablo to stop blackmailing him. So, he wants to scare Pablo."

"You think Fred killed Sasha?" asked Beanie.

"Certainly possible," said Joshua. "Maybe to keep her quiet. Maybe he got rid of one blackmailer only to gain another one."

"Well, I think there's only one thing left to do," said Beanie.

Joshua nodded. "We need to talk to Fred Zachary."

42

"Fred killed Sasha Hidalgo," said Mrs. Zachary, wringing her hands as she paced back and forth in the small sitting room where she'd invited Beanie and Joshua to sit.

When they rang the doorbell of the Zachary villa minutes ago, the housekeeper had told them Mr. Zachary wasn't home, but as she was closing the door, Mrs. Zachary appeared in the foyer and ushered them inside, almost as if she'd been expecting their visit.

"Why do you think that?" asked Beanie.

Dressed in a flowing silk caftan that billowed behind her as she paced, Mrs. Zachary said, "First, you should know this: I hired Pablo Lima to get evidence against Fred."

"Why did you do that?" asked Joshua.

The woman gave Joshua an annoyed look. "Obviously, I suspected Fred of cheating on me. I needed proof so I could divorce him, leave him penniless, and move on with my life."

"And Pablo gave you the proof of Fred's infidelity?" asked Beanie.

Mrs. Zachary nodded. "However, during Pablo's investigation into my husband, he and I would often meet in secret. I believe Fred caught me whispering with Pablo a few times, even though I tried to be discreet."

"And so Fred thought you were fooling around with Pablo," said Beanie, recalling Fred Zachary's belligerent behavior at the pool, when he'd confronted Pablo, actions which caused his removal from the area. Now it made sense why Fred Zachary had accused his wife of flirting with Pablo Lima.

Joshua said, "Okay, obviously, Fred had a motive to kill Pablo. But, what makes you think he killed Sasha? Why would he do that?"

"Because Sasha also knew that Fred was cheating on me," said Mrs. Zachary.

Confused, Beanie asked, "She did?"

Mrs. Zachary said, "After Sasha confronted me about cheating with Pablo, I set the record straight and told her I'd hired Pablo, and Pablo confirmed with Sasha that he was getting evidence on Fred. I'm certain Sasha knew everything Pablo knew."

"But are you certain that Fred knew Sasha knew about the proof of him cheating on you?" asked Joshua.

Good question, thought Beanie. One he wanted to know the answer to.

Blinking, her face a mask of uncertainty, Mrs. Zachary paused for a moment but then waved her hand dismissively. "Fred must have found out somehow. Maybe Pablo told him. Or, maybe Fred assumed because Pablo and Sasha were a couple."

Not convinced by Mrs. Zachary's logic, but not inclined to dispute it at the moment, Beanie asked, "Any idea how Fred would have gotten snake venom?"

Mrs. Zachary pressed two fingers against the bridge of her nose. "I have no idea. But it fits the way Fred does things, considering the way his ex-wives died."

"But with his first wife," said Joshua, "it was antifreeze poisoning. Not snake venom."

"Fred was very resourceful," said Mrs. Zachary. "If he wanted snake venom, I have no doubt that he could have gotten his hands on some. But, look, I want to give you the proof Pablo secured for me. I keep it in a safe deposit box at my bank in town. I'll go there today and get it, then email it to you."

Ten minutes later, walking away from the Zachary villa, Beanie asked, "You agree with Mrs. Zachary? You think Fred killed Pablo and Sasha?"

Joshua sighed. "He could have, but I don't know. Guess I'm just hung up on how he could have gotten the snake venom."

"You don't think Sasha could have given it to him?" asked Beanie. "That's what we came up with when we spoke with PJ."

"Yeah, I know, but …"

"But?" prompted Beanie as they headed across the courtyard, then stepped onto the wide pedestrian path leading toward the main road that snaked through the resort.

"But the more I think about it," said Joshua. "The more I can't imagine Fred and Sasha plotting together."

"It seems unlikely," agreed Beanie. "But stranger things have happened. And at the end of the day, if Marcus isn't the killer and Fred didn't do it, then … who did?"

43

"You need to come to the paper now," said Joshua, excitement in his tone. "You are not going to believe this."

"What's going on?" asked Beanie, pouring a second cup of coffee into his mug.

He could only think there'd been some sort of development in the Pablo Lima or Sasha Hidalgo murder investigation. And if so, then what a difference a day makes seemed an appropriate cliché. Yesterday afternoon, following the conversation with Mrs. Zachary, Joshua went back to the *Aerie Observer* while Beanie headed to the Bronson villa.

There he checked in with his boss, then took a swim to clear his mind, and a nap to calm his nerves. He woke up to a phone call from Noelle, then spent a few hours video chatting with the boys. After a late dinner, he went to bed.

Joshua said, "No, I can't tell you over the phone."

Beanie scowled. "Why not?"

"You literally need to see this to believe it," insisted Joshua.

Sighing his frustration, Beanie said, "Give me half an hour."

Forty-five minutes later, sitting in the guest chair in Joshua's cubicle, Beanie asked, "Okay, what do I need to see to believe?"

"This morning, Mrs. Zachary emailed me the proof Pablo Lima gave her about Fred cheating," said Joshua, turning to his computer. "A series of photographs. Fred and his secret girlfriend fooling around when they thought no one was looking."

"Who's the secret girlfriend?" asked Beanie.

"One second," said Joshua, making a few clicks with his mouse. A moment later, the printer beneath his desk came to life, humming loudly, spitting out a document. Joshua grabbed the paper, and swiveled in his chair to face Beanie.

"Let me see it," said Beanie.

His gaze slightly mischievous, Joshua said, "Brace yourself."

"Just give me the paper."

Joshua handed it over.

Beanie stared at the color copy.

The former intern had given him good advice. Beanie should have braced himself.

"What on earth?"

"My thoughts exactly," said Joshua.

Rocked with confusion, Beanie gaped at the photo of Fred Zachary kissing Daisy Cox.

"I'm feeling much better about Fred Zachary as the main suspect," said Joshua. "He had a strong motive to kill both Pablo and Sasha. They both knew he was cheating with Daisy."

Beanie lifted his gaze from the photo, which looked like a bad accident, something both repulsive and compelling. "You think Pablo told Sasha about Fred cheating with Daisy?"

Joshua shrugged. "Or, maybe Daisy told Sasha herself. Or, maybe Sasha knew, then told Pablo and helped him get the proof of Fred's infidelity."

Nodding, Beanie said, "What about the snake venom?"

"I'm inclined to believe what Mrs. Zachary said," Joshua told him. "Fred is wealthy, powerful, and well-connected. He's a friend of the zoo. People like him find ways to get what they want."

Beanie stroked his chin. "And maybe the snake venom is kind of genius, you know? He picks a poison that he seemingly has no access to."

"Right," said Joshua, leaning back in his chair. "But I gotta tell you. Fred Zachary and Daisy Cox?"

"You were right," said Beanie. "Something you have to see to believe."

"Wonder what she sees in that old guy?" asked Joshua.

"Daisy doesn't strike me as the most self-assured girl," said Beanie.

Joshua frowned. "You think Fred groomed her?"

"There's some type of power imbalance at play," said Beanie. "And it's in Fred's favor. And possibly to Daisy's detriment. If Daisy doesn't think much of herself, then Fred could have been able to fool her with lots of attention and affection. Daisy could have taken Fred's behavior to heart when she shouldn't have."

"I take it you don't think they're in love?" asked Joshua.

"It's possible, but I doubt it."

Nodding, Joshua said, "Well, we need to see what Fred has to say for himself."

44

"You think Fred Zachary will talk to us?" Joshua asked.

"I'm sure he'll curse at us and slam the door in our faces," said Beanie, walking alongside the former intern as they headed along the pathway toward the Zachary villa.

"Then why bother?"

"Because you need to confront him with these allegations," said Beanie. "And if he says no comment, then you write that. But, you have to give the subject of the story a heads up so they have an opportunity to refute it, should they want to."

"Yeah, that's true," conceded Joshua. "But I'm sure Fred Zachary will deny having an affair with Daisy."

"But, we have proof," said Beanie, ducking beneath the low-hanging branches of a guava tree. "Those photos of Fred and Daisy will be hard to deny."

As they rounded the corner and came abreast of the private road leading to the Zachary villa, Beanie frowned.

"What's going on?" asked Joshua, slowing to a stop.

Beanie shook his head, trying to make sense of the scene before him.

Roughly forty feet ahead, a half dozen police cars, red and blue lights flashing, formed a haphazard semi-circle around the villa's large courtyard. Several cops stood near the home's grand entrance. In addition to the police, dozens of resort guests stood on the perimeter pedestrian pathways, their faces shocked and concerned.

"What could have happened," wondered Beanie.

"I don't know, but I see a guy from the force that I talk to regularly," Joshua said. "Let's go find out."

Five minutes later, Beanie, Joshua, and a police officer named Montez stood near the back of the squad car. Closer to the action, the scene was more chaotic. In addition to incessant chatter from the police radios, there was the din of hushed conversation among the onlookers, and a hollow, plaintive wailing. The wretched sound floated out in the steamy mid-morning humidity from the villa's front doors, which were opened.

"What's that noise?" asked Beanie.

Officer Montez glanced over his shoulder at the villa, then said, "Mrs. Zachary."

"Is she okay?" asked Joshua.

"Doubt it," said Montez, an islander of medium height and build. "My understanding is she found him."

"She found who?" asked Beanie, his heart starting to pound.

"Her husband," said Montez, his expression grim.

"Fred Zachary?" asked Joshua. "What happened to him?"

"He's dead," said Montez. "Stabbed about a dozen times, is my understanding."

Beanie's head swam. Fred Zachary. Dead. What was going on? How was Fred Zachary dead?

Joshua asked, "Did she kill him?"

An appropriate question, thought Beanie, considering the woman had been aware of her husband's infidelity.

Montez shrugged. "Not sure. She's been wailing and screaming since we got here. It's either grief or a good act. She'll be taken to the station. Detectives will figure it out."

"What did she tell the first responders?" Joshua asked.

"She was pretty incoherent," Montez said. "Just kept saying he's dead, my husband is dead. Wouldn't answer any questions. Or maybe couldn't. Hey, I need to get back. But give me a call tomorrow. I might know more."

After Montez walked away, Beanie took a deep breath. "I don't even know what to think."

"How about who did it," said Joshua, shaking his head. "What do you think about that?"

"Honestly," said Beanie, glancing toward the villa where cops and crime scene techs walked in and out of the house. "I have no idea."

"I think it was Mrs. Zachary," said Joshua.

Beanie frowned. "I know she wanted a divorce. I didn't think she wanted him dead."

"I don't think she wanted him dead," said Joshua. "I wonder if maybe she was defending herself."

"What do you mean?"

"Like you said, she wanted a divorce," said Joshua. "Obviously, Fred didn't want to be left penniless, which was her plan. Maybe they argued."

Beanie nodded. "He's a confrontational type of guy."

Joshua said, "And I can see Fred Zachary maybe getting physical with his wife."

"So you think Fred attacked her?"

"It's possible," said Joshua. "And then to save her life, Mrs. Zachary had no choice but to kill her husband."

45

"Mr. Bean?" said the timid, plaintive voice, barely above a whisper. "It's Daisy Cox."

"Daisy?" echoed Beanie, curious and concerned.

Eight hours had passed since Fred Zachary had been stabbed to death in his villa. After leaving the crime scene, Joshua returned to the *Aerie Observer* while Beanie made plans for a late lunch with Carmen and Marcus Taylor.

Mother and son were much more hopeful, now that it seemed the police would most likely drop the charges against Marcus. Beanie caught them up on the details of his investigation with Joshua, and they speculated about who the murderer could be, now that Fred Zachary was dead.

Although Carmen still believed Fred was responsible. As she pointed out, the man's death didn't mean he hadn't been a murderer himself. Following lunch, Beanie returned to the Bronson villa, video-chatted with Noelle and the boys, took a swim, and a nap.

He'd woken up an hour ago, a bit hungry, and was in the kitchen, scanning the refrigerator contents, when his mobile rang.

"I'd like to talk to you," said Daisy.

"Talk to me about what?"

"About what happened to … Mr. Zachary."

"He was found dead," said Beanie, recalling what he'd learned about Daisy and Fred Zachary. The photos of the unlikely May-December pair filled his mind. "The police think someone murdered him."

"I … " Daisy's hoarse whisper trailed off into a gasping sob.

"What?"

"I … I know who killed Fred."

"What are you talking about?" asked Beanie, a frisson of doubt snaking through him. "You know who killed Fred Zachary?"

Sniffing, Daisy said, "That's what I need to talk to you about. I need to tell you who killed him …"

"Who was it?"

"Can we talk in person?" asked Daisy. "Can you meet me?"

The doubt turned to alarm. Something in Daisy's voice, the hitch of hesitation, made him think she was in trouble. Made him wonder if she was in danger. If she knew who killed Fred Zachary, then maybe the murderer knew that, as well. Considering her secret dalliance with Zachary, Beanie wondered if Daisy had been with the man when he was stabbed to death.

What if Daisy didn't just know who killed Fred?

What if Daisy had seen who'd killed Fred?

The fragile, timid girl might have been present when Fred had been attacked. A secret tryst with Fred might have turned deadly. Daisy could have fled the Zachary villa in terror, fearful for her life.

Had Fred's killer threatened her?

Or worse, was the killer there with her, right now, forcing her to call him?

A chill passed through Beanie. Something similar happened to Joshua. The former intern was kidnapped and made to call his friends and loved ones, telling them he was okay. And nothing had been further from the truth.

His heart pounding, Beanie said, "Where are you?"

"I'm at my aunt's house," she said.

"Where Joshua and I visited you?" confirmed Beanie, grabbing the keys to the SUV, and heading down the long, wide hallway leading to the foyer.

"Right," said Daisy. "Can you come, please? I'm … I'm really scared."

"Have you called the police?"

"Please, you are the only one who can help me!"

Beanie said, "Give me twenty minutes."

46

In the balmy, jasmine-scented night air, Beanie opened the door of the SUV, climbed inside, and—

Something in the rear-view mirror caught his attention. Beanie glanced at the backseat. A shudder passed through him as he froze, confused. What on earth? Twisting in the bucket seat, he stared at Joshua Howard. The former intern slouched in the seat behind him, eyes closed, head lolled to the side.

"Joshua … " said Beanie, unable to fathom what was happening as he heard a sound that nearly paralyzed him.

The unmistakable metallic slide of a gun being racked.

Fear gripped him as his mind traveled back to the past when he'd been kidnapped by a group of thugs who'd thrown a black hood over his head and forced him into a car. Was that happening again? Was he being kidnapped? But, why? Who would want to—

"Do exactly what I say and you won't get killed."

Beanie frowned.

He recognized the voice. But, it didn't make sense …

"Daisy …" Beanie was beyond confused. Why was Daisy here? He was just talking to her. She'd told him she was at her aunt's house.

"Mr. Bean," said Daisy, her voice low and menacing.

"What are you doing?"

"What I'm doing is *not* blowing your head off," said Daisy. "But I will if you don't do exactly what I tell you."

"What do you want me to do?" asked Beanie, struggling to think, to figure out what was happening, to find a way to escape.

"Handcuff yourself," said Daisy. "And then get into the backseat."

Beanie glanced at her. "What—"

A pair of metal cuffs landed on his lap.

Staring at the shackles, Beanie shook his head. "I'm not doing it."

"Excuse me?"

"I'm not handcuffing myself," said Beanie, glaring at Daisy. "Why should I? You're going to kill me anyway, right? Like you killed Joshua."

"He's not dead," she snapped. "But he knows how to follow instructions. When I told him to cuff himself and get in the backseat, he didn't hesitate."

Beanie glanced at the cuffs again.

Why would Daisy want him to handcuff himself if she planned to kill him? She didn't need him to be restrained to put a bullet in him. So what was her plan? Why did she want him to get in the backseat? Did she want the cops to find two dead bodies in the SUV? What was the deranged woman's endgame?

Beanie had no idea.

But maybe doing her twisted bidding was the only way to find out. And the best way to stay alive.

47

Ten minutes later, Beanie sat in the backseat of the SUV, his handcuffed wrists resting on his lap.

As soon as he'd secured the shackles, something within rebelled. His wife and boys flashed before his eyes. Memories of other times when he'd been in danger assailed him, a vicious mental assault that quelled the rebellion and brought about self-recrimination. Massive regret. How many times had he promised his wife that he wouldn't end up in yet another life-or-death situation? How many times did he think he was going to make it out alive? Wasn't his luck going to run out?

Shaking away the morbid thoughts, Beanie glanced at Joshua, still slumped in the seat next to him.

Daisy hadn't lied. Joshua was breathing, his chest slowly rising and falling. An unexpected surge of pride welled within Beanie. His former intern had done a great job of investigating Pablo Lima's murder. Joshua's articles had been precise, thorough, and engaging. Many had trended, so much that Joshua's social media following was growing.

Would he get a chance to tell Joshua that he was shaping up to be a great reporter?

Again, Beanie shook away the depressing thoughts. He and Joshua had been in a life-or-death situation together before. They'd survived then. Beanie had to believe they would survive this night.

As the SUV followed the coastal road, its headlights illuminating the strip of concrete, Beanie glanced at Daisy through the rearview mirror.

The disturbed woman stared straight ahead, affording him a limited view of her face. But he could see her hands, clutched in a death grip around the steering wheel.

Beanie still didn't know what to think of Daisy Cox. How had she fooled him? How had he not suspected her?

Once he and Joshua learned about her affair with Fred Zachary, they should have put her on the suspect list. Obviously, she had a motive to kill Pablo. The good-looking lifeguard was blackmailing her secret boyfriend. Beanie wouldn't have been surprised if Fred hadn't convinced Daisy to kill Pablo. Daisy had access to the snake venom, because of Sasha, and proximity to Pablo. How easy would it have been for Daisy to poison the scotch?

And as for killing Sasha, Daisy, and Fred could have been getting rid of loose ends. Or, maybe, Sasha found out that Daisy stole the snake venom that Pablo hadn't been able to sell. Or maybe Sasha decided to blackmail Fred Zachary, as well. After all, Sasha probably knew about the affair between Daisy and Fred, so—

"You're awfully quiet back there, Mr. Bean," said Daisy. "I hope you're not doing anything stupid like trying to get out of those handcuffs."

Beanie glanced in the rearview mirror.

Daisy was looking back at him, her gaze fierce and intense.

"Just remember I've got this gun on my lap," she said. "I know how to use it, and I will."

"Where are we going?" asked Beanie, hoping their voices might rouse Joshua. If the former intern was awake, maybe the two of them could come up with a way to escape.

From the driver's seat, Daisy said, "I need your help with something."

"My help?" asked Beanie,

"You were right, Mr. Bean," said Daisy. "I am going to kill you. And

Joshua, too. But, I'm not getting arrested or going to jail for your murders. Marcus will be doing that."

"I don't understand," said Beanie, though it was obvious Daisy had let Marcus take the blame for the deaths of Pablo and Sasha.

"We need to get evidence that will make the cops think Marcus killed you and Joshua," said Daisy.

"That doesn't make any sense," said Beanie. "Why would Marcus kill me? Or Joshua? We were trying to help him clear his name."

"And in doing so," said Daisy, "you discovered that Marcus is a cold-blooded murderer. He kills you so you won't give the police the evidence which shows he killed Pablo, Sasha, and Fred."

Beanie scoffed. "So, Marcus is some kind of serial killer, is that what you want the police to think?"

"That's right."

"And how is that supposed to work?"

"You know, Mr. Bean, you ask a lot of questions," said Daisy.

Picking up on the slight shrillness in her tone, Beanie said, "I'm a journalist."

Daisy said nothing, but Beanie sensed the SUV increasing in speed. His heart pounding, Beanie glanced at the speedometer. The needle moved steadily to the right. On the road ahead, Daisy accelerated toward the back of the vehicle in front of the SUV, then jerked the car to the right as she sped around to pass it.

"Did you kill Pablo Lima because he was blackmailing Fred?" asked Beanie.

"Again with those questions," said Daisy, her tone clipped, curt.

"Well, I'm curious," said Beanie. "And since you're going to kill me anyway, what does it matter if I know the truth?"

"The truth is that Pablo Lima was an evil, deceitful, manipulative thief who deserved to die," said Daisy, grinding the words through gritted teeth.

"Because he blackmailed Fred?"

"He was only able to blackmail Fred because Mrs. Zachary hired him to snoop around in Fred's business, where he did not belong," said Daisy. "And Pablo didn't even need to blackmail Fred. Mrs. Zachary paid him for those photos Pablo took of me and Fred. But Pablo was just so vile and disgusting and money-hungry."

"So you killed him?"

Daisy laughed, a disturbing, maniacal sound. "Probably one of the easiest things I've ever done. Pablo was also stealing Fred's scotch. So, I figured I would spike the scotch with snake venom."

"How did you do that?"

"Me, Sasha, Marcus, and Pablo went to the Zachary villa the day Pablo crashed Sasha's car. Once inside, Pablo told Marcus to get a bottle of scotch from Fred's liquor cabinet, which he did. Then we all took turns taking a few swigs. This was Pablo's custom. He would let us have a taste, then the rest was for him. Then, Marcus took the bottle back into the house and returned to the pool. We spent some time out there, and then I told the others I had to use the little girl's room. But, I really didn't. I went into the house and put the snake venom into the scotch. Then I wiped all the prints off the bottle and went back to the pool. After a while, we decided to leave before Fred or his nagging fishwife came back. Although, it didn't matter because Marcus had told us Mrs. Zachary would sometimes erase the surveillance tapes that showed us in their villa. That's why Sasha thought Pablo and Mrs. Zachary were fooling around. The truth was, Pablo was working for Mrs. Zachary. Getting evidence against Fred."

"Where did you get the venom?"

"That was venom Sasha had stolen a year ago," said Daisy. "Honestly, I wasn't even sure it was still effective. I mean, what's the expiration date on black mamba venom? Is there one? Anyway, I figured I would find out. And I did. Of course, Pablo didn't die right away."

"Did Sasha know you took the venom she stole?"

"Not at first," said Daisy. "But, after it came out that Pablo died from venom poisoning, she started getting suspicious of me. And then, when she couldn't find the venom, she confronted me about it. I denied it, but I was the only other person besides Pablo who knew about the stolen venom. She kept questioning me. And I tried to accuse her of killing Pablo, but she got in my face and threatened to tell the cops her suspicions. I had to kill her."

As Daisy sped up and passed another car, Beanie asked, "Did Fred tell you to kill Pablo?"

Daisy scoffed. "Are you serious? Fred had no idea what I did for him. He was freaking out about Pablo blackmailing him. Kept telling him that his wife would leave him broke if she found out about us. He wanted to try and scare Pablo into backing off. Wanted to hire some guy to beat him up."

The exiled PC-5 gang member, Beanie recalled.

"I knew that wasn't going to work," said Daisy. "Pablo wasn't the type to scare easily. I knew something permanent had to be done. The only way Pablo would stop blackmailing Fred was if Pablo was dead."

"And so the blackmailing stopped?" asked Beanie.

"Not that Fred appreciated it," said Daisy, a hitch of hurt in her voice as it rose in pitch. "He didn't realize what I'd done for him. Done for us. When I told him, he pulled away from me. Looked at me with this disgust and shock and horror. Him? A man who'd killed his two ex-wives. He stared at me as though I were vile and repulsive. And then he told me that it was over between us …"

"Fred ended your relationship?"

Daisy Cox said, "And I ended Fred …"

48

An ice-cold jolt sliced through Beanie.

And I ended Fred.

Had Daisy just said that? Had she confessed to killing Fred Zachary?

Beanie opened his mouth, intending to ask a question, but movement in his periphery made him pause.

He glanced over.

Joshua's manacled hands, held chest high, were moving.

The former intern was staring at him, holding a finger against his lips. Beanie recognized that Joshua didn't want him to let Daisy know that he was awake. Beanie gave a slow nod of acknowledgment. Joshua responded by pointing his fingers toward the cup holder in the bucket seat. In the dark interior of the car, Beanie could make out a smartphone resting in the receptacle.

Questions swirled in Beanie's mind. Where had the phone come from? Was it Joshua's? if so, had it come from his pocket? How had he managed to get it out? When had he managed to get it out?

But the most important question was, how could they use it?

Beanie didn't think it would be impossible to use the phone, if he was able to maneuver his wrists in the right position, but wouldn't Daisy eventually notice?

Joshua pointed toward the driver's seat. Beanie assumed he was indicating something about Daisy. Then Joshua made the informal sign for talking, tapping his fingertips against his thumb. Daisy. Talking. Did the former intern want him to keep Daisy talking?

Figuring Joshua would somehow, someway, try to use the smartphone to alert the police, Beanie said, "You killed Fred. I thought you loved him."

"I did love him," said Daisy. "I thought he loved me, too. But he turned on me."

"How did you even get involved with Fred Zachary?" asked Beanie, careful to keep his eyes on the rearview mirror, even though, next to him, he sensed Joshua's slight, furtive movements. He didn't want Daisy to check the rear view and find him glancing in Joshua's direction.

Beanie wished he knew what the former intern was planning but he would trust it was some scheme to get them out of their current predicament alive.

"Isn't he old enough to be your father?" asked Beanie.

"So what?" snapped Daisy. "Age doesn't matter. Maturity is more important. Most guys my age are ignorant and reckless. All they want to do is party and hook up with as many girls as possible. Pablo was like that. Marcus is like that. PJ is like that. They're all like that."

"But Fred was different."

"Fred was my emotional and intellectual equal," said Daisy, her voice whispery and dreamlike. "He really understood me. He listened to me. And he heard me. He made me feel beautiful and special. He cared about me like no other man has, not even my own father."

"Maybe that's why you liked Fred," suggested Beanie. "Maybe he was the father figure you needed—"

"Oh, shut up!" barked Daisy. "You sound like Sasha! Accusing me of having daddy issues. Well, maybe I did. Because, in the end, Fred turned out to be just like my dad. Fred betrayed me. After everything I did for him."

"So you stabbed him to death," said Beanie.

"I really didn't want to," said Daisy. "But Fred said it was over. It wasn't going to work between us anymore. His wife was divorcing him and she had proof of our love. That meant Fred wouldn't get any alimony in the divorce. We would have no money to live on, he told me. I tried to tell him that I have a job and he could get a job, but he didn't want to listen. And that's when I told him everything I'd done for him."

"You told him about Pablo and Sasha."

"I tried to explain that he didn't have to worry about being blackmailed because I had gotten rid of Pablo," said Daisy. "But, as I said, he thought I was psycho. He started telling me that he wasn't going to have the cops thinking that he and I had plotted to kill Pablo together. He said he wasn't going to prison for me. And it was then that I realized he had lied to me … he never loved me. He told me to leave. But I didn't. I went to the kitchen, got a knife, and went back upstairs. He was in the shower, washing off traces of me, I suppose. I stabbed him. Over and over. And, for a second, I got a memory of this movie I watched with my aunt when I was younger. A woman got stabbed in the shower. It was an old black and white movie."

"Psycho …" supplied Beanie.

Daisy laughed. "Yeah, that's—"

Joshua launched his body up, looped his arms over the headrest, and pressed his shackled wrists against Daisy's throat.

Beanie cried out as the SUV jerked to the left, and then whipped back to the right as Daisy twisted the steering wheel back and forth with one hand. Unable to grab on to anything, he was tossed back and forth and from side to side, as though he were in an out-of-control carnival ride, powerless to stop his momentum as the vehicle careened and fishtail from one side of the road to the other.

Clawing at Joshua's arms with her free hand, Daisy screamed and cursed.

Feeling useless and helpless, Beanie struggled to thrust his shackled hands between the bucket seats, thinking he might be able to, somehow, someway, push the ignition button and stall the car. But it was no use. Joshua and Daisy panted and grunted, both of them desperate to get the advantage. Joshua kept his hands against Daisy's neck while Daisy let go of the wheel and tried to scratch at Joshua's face, clawing at his nose and eyes, trying to force him to release his hold.

The SUV drifted into oncoming traffic.

"We're going to crash head-on!" shouted Beanie as horns blared in protest and headlights danced in his eyes, blinding him. Lowering his lids, Beanie twisted his head from the harsh glare. Sirens wailed in the distance, becoming louder and louder. Beanie opened his eyes and looked over his shoulder. Several police squad cars sped toward the SUV. Flashing red and blue lights flooded the car's dim interior. Seconds later, one of the cop cars pulled alongside the SUV. The car shook and then the police car rammed the SUV. The force caused Beanie to slide against the passenger door as the car's tires skidded.

Beanie's mind was a whirl of confusion as the SUV spun out of control. Chassis rocking, the car bounced from side to side as it slammed into a tree. The airbags deployed, releasing a fine powdery mist.

Pulling his looped arms over the headrest, Joshua collapsed into the backseat as Daisy fell forward against the airbag.

Doors opened and slammed.

Footsteps pounded the pavement as officers shouted commands.

Relieved, his heart slamming, Beanie slumped in his seat …

EPILOGUE

"As my wife would say, we could have been killed," said Beanie, taking a sip of coffee.

At eight in the morning, Beanie was still feeling edgy and wired from the previous night's chaotic events, which Joshua had furiously chronicled in an online article that dropped after midnight, and immediately began to trend.

"Okay, so it wasn't my best move," Joshua admitted, swiveling from his computer to face Beanie. "But I had to do something."

"Yeah, but I didn't expect you to do that," said Beanie, recalling the former intern's wild attempt at choking Daisy Cox.

Shrugging, Joshua said, "Well, what else could I do? My hands were tied."

"Touché," said Beanie, holding up his coffee cup in a mock salute. "But I thought you were going to call the cops."

"Yeah, so did I," said Joshua. "But once I managed to get my phone from my pocket, I realized calling anyone would tip off Daisy. She would hear the person saying hello and realize that she hadn't knocked me unconscious like she assumed she had."

"True," agreed Beanie.

"Instead, I managed to activate my recording app," said Joshua, smiling.

"Which the police appreciated," said Beanie. "A pretty genius move."

"They probably won't be able to use it in court," lamented Joshua. "But, it was enough to question her and she caved, so …"

Beanie took another sip of coffee.

After the car crash, Daisy Cox had been arrested and taken to the police station. During her interrogation, the recording of her ranting confession was played for her. According to Joshua's girlfriend Friday, Daisy didn't deny her murderous rampage but blamed her actions on her victims, who she claimed abused, misused, and deceived her.

"The latest update from Fri," said Joshua, "is that Daisy plans to use self-defense."

Beanie gaped at Joshua. "Are you kidding?"

Nodding, Joshua said, "She claims that Pablo, Sasha, and Fred mentally abused her which caused her to harm them physically."

"She actually thinks a jury will believe that?"

"Who knows?" Joshua shook his head.

"Well, you'll be busy with her case for a few months," said Beanie.

"And my podcast," Joshua said.

"Podcast?"

"My editor thinks I should do a podcast about Daisy," said Joshua, rapt enthusiasm in his gaze. "I think it's a good idea, too. I have a ton of notes about the story. Lots of stuff I had to leave out of the articles. There are a lot of themes and angles and perspectives."

"Sounds interesting," said Beanie, standing. "But, I'm not interested."

"Why not?" Joshua chuckled. "Come on, you have to let me interview you. The listeners will want to hear from my mentor. The person who guided me in the right direction, toward the truth, as I conducted my investigation."

"We'll see," said Beanie, though he was secretly pleased that Joshua appreciated his guidance. "But, right now, what I have to do is get home to my wife and my kids and—"

"The next crime you have to cover," said Joshua.

"Yeah, that too," agreed Beanie, scratching his chin. "I'm pretty sure that while I was on vacation, somebody in St. Killian was committing cold-blooded murder ...”

Did that mystery have more twists and turns than an island coastal highway, or what?

And poor Beanie!

All he wanted to do was enjoy his vacation and, wouldn't you know it, he got caught up in another murder mystery!

At least, this time, he got to play mentor to his former intern, Joshua and helped him track down the killer.

Speaking of the murderer, who would have suspected snake venom as a murder weapon! Quite an interesting choice of poison!

Well, unfortunately, summer vacation is over and Beanie has to get back to work.

And a new year will bring a new mystery!

Should auld acquaintance be forgot,
And never brought to mind?

Beanie will certainly want to forget the man who shows up in his backyard after midnight on New Year's Eve, bleeding from a stab wound!

When the man utters a name, it seems the victim has identified the person who stabbed him.

But, as Beanie investigates the case, he discovers the man had many secrets and even more enemies ...

Happy New Year Murder is the next holiday cozy mystery novel in the Reporter Roland Bean Cozy Mystery series. With plenty of twists and turns, it will keep you guessing until the jaw-dropping ending that you won't see coming!

Get your copy of Happy New Year Murder today!
https://geni.us/happynewyearmurder

Are you eagerly anticipating Beanie's next unexpected detour into a mystery waiting to be solved?

Then **Beanie's Mini Mystery Moments** are for you!

Get an exclusive quick-read mystery that spins off from one of Beanie's mystery adventures delivered straight to your email inbox!
https://BookHip.com/RLJNAJA

ALSO BY RACHEL WOODS

SASSY SARCASTIC CAT COZY MYSTERIES

Sophie Carter, a struggling reporter for the *Palmchat Gazette*, teams up with a sassy talking Calico cat to solve crimes as she strives to become an influential investigative reporter

A SLY AND SINISTER TAIL

A COLD AND CALCULATING TAIL

A FOUL AND FRIGHTENING TAIL

A DARK AND DEVIOUS TAIL

REPORTER ROLAND BEAN COZY MYSTERIES

Roland "Beanie" Bean, husband and loving father, finds himself the unwitting participant in solving crimes as he seeks to make a name for himself as a reporter for the *Palmchat Gazette*.

HAPPY BIRTHDAY MURDER

EASTER EGG HUNT MURDER

MERRY CHRISTMAS MURDER

TRICK OR TREAT MURDER

GOBBLE GOBBLE MURDER

HAPPY 4TH OF JULY MURDER

SUMMER VACATION MURDER

HAPPY NEW YEAR MURDER

PALMCHAT ISLANDS MYSTERIES

Married journalists, Vivian and Leo, manage the island newspaper while solving crimes as they chase leads for their next story.

UNTIL DEATH DO US PART

NO ONE WILL FIND YOU

YOU WILL DIE FOR THIS

DON'T MAKE ME HURT YOU

THE PALMCHAT ISLANDS MYSTERIES BOX SET: BOOKS 1 - 4

RUTHLESS REVENGE ROMANCE SERIES

Gripping romantic suspense series with steamy romance, unpredictable plot twists and devastating consequences of deceit.

HER DEADLY MISTAKE

HER DEADLY DECEPTION

HER DEADLY THREAT

HER DEADLY BETRAYAL

MURDER IN PARADISE SERIES

A series of stand-alone women sleuth mysteries with murder, mayhem and a dash of romance, set against the backdrop of turquoise waters and swaying palm trees of the fictional Palmchat Islands.

THE UNWORTHY WIFE

THE SILENT ENEMY

THE PERFECT LIAR

ABOUT THE AUTHOR

Rachel Woods studied journalism and graduated from the University of Houston where she published articles in the Daily Cougar. She is a legal assistant by day and a freelance writer and blogger with a penchant for melodrama by night. Many of her stories take place on the islands, which she has visited around the world. Rachel resides in Houston, Texas with her three sock monkeys.

For more information:
www.therachelwoods.com
rachel@therachelwoods.com

ABOUT THE PUBLISHER

 **BONZAIMOON BOOKS**

BonzaiMoon Books is a family-run, artisanal publishing company created in the summer of 2014. We publish works of fiction in various genres. Our passion and focus is working with authors who write the books you want to read, and giving those authors the opportunity to have more direct input in the publishing of their work.

For more information:
www.bonzaimoonbooks.com
info@bonzaimoonbooks.com